MIDDLE SCHOOL
Master of Disaster

JAMES PATTERSON is the internationally bestselling author of the highly praised Middle School books, *Not So Normal Norbert*, *Unbelievably Boring Bart*, *Katt vs. Dogg* and the I Funny, Jacky Ha-Ha, Treasure Hunters, Dog Diaries and Max Einstein series. James Patterson's books have sold more than 385 million copies worldwide, making him one of the biggest-selling authors of all time. He lives in Florida.

CHRIS TEBBETTS has collaborated with James Patterson on nine books in the Middle School series as well as *Kenny Wright: Superhero*, and he is also the author of the Viking Saga, a fantasy adventure series for young readers. He lives in Vermont.

A list of titles by James Patterson
appears at the back of this book

MIDDLE SCHOOL
Master of Disaster

JAMES PATTERSON

AND CHRIS TEBBETTS

ILLUSTRATED BY JOMIKE TEJIDO

1 3 5 7 9 10 8 6 4 2

Young Arrow
20 Vauxhall Bridge Road
London SW1V 2SA

Young Arrow is part of the Penguin Random House group of companies
whose addresses can be found at global.penguinrandomhouse.com

Penguin
Random House
UK

First published in Great Britain by Young Arrow in 2020

www.penguin.co.uk

A CIP catalogue record for this book is available
from the British Library

ISBN 9781529119534

Printed and bound in Great Britain by Clays Ltd, Elcograf S.p.A.

Penguin Random House is committed to a sustainable future
for our business, our readers and our planet. This book is made
from Forest Stewardship Council® certified paper.

MIX
Paper from
responsible sources
FSC® C018179

FOR MS. ALWON AND
ALL OF HER STUDENTS AT
JEFFERSON ACADEMY

—CT

MIDDLE SCHOOL
Master of Disaster

CHAPTER 1

WHAT'S THE STORY?

CHAPTER 2

WELCOME, WELCOME!

 **M**an, have I got a story for you!
Actually, scratch that. I have a whole bunch of stories, but let me catch you up first.

You might be wondering who I am and why I'm here. Well, this whole thing started after I recently put together my own book company. People said I'd never pull *that* off, and when I did, I thought, *Why not keep going?* So when my friend Max Einstein suggested putting on the world's biggest show to get every kid in America excited about books, stories, and reading, I was all about it.

So I got together an amazing team of storytellers, including our friend Rafe Khatchadorian.

I pulled a few strings and booked some awesome musical guests.

I filled out about two tons of paperwork and got permission to use the National Mall in Washington, DC.

Then we all worked for months to spread the word and bring the whole thing together.

And guess what? It was actually happening!

By the time I got up on stage that day, we had about ten thousand people on the National Mall, not to mention another zillion watching on their TVs, computers, and phones across the country. Standing there in front of all those people and cameras, I felt about as nervous as a goldfish at a shark family reunion.

But you didn't come here to listen to me talk about this stuff. You came for the show. You came for the *stories,* just like everyone else. So let's get to it.

"Okay, everyone!" I said, and my voice boomed out over the National Mall. "You might have heard of our first storyteller from books like *Middle School, The Worst Years of My Life,* or movies like...well...*Middle School, The Worst Years of My Life.* Some people might call him a world-class troublemaker, but he's pretty awesome at telling stories, too. So make some noise for my friend—the kid, the myth, the legend in his own hometown... Rafe Khatchadorian! Take it away, Rafe!"

CHAPTER 3

DEEP SPACE, DEEPER TROUBLE

 **F**irst of all, let me tell you that everything in this story really happened. It's just that some of it happened in my real life, and some of it happened in my imagination.

Don't say I didn't warn you.

So there I am one day, speeding along the edge of the galaxy in my one-man FTL cruiser. I've got the thrusters maxed out, way past the speed of light, and I'm passing planets, wormholes, supernovas, and space trash like they're snails along the highway.

No big deal. Just an average Tuesday afternoon in deep space...right up until my navigation alert system lights up like an intergalactic Christmas tree.

"Warning!" says a robotic voice. "You are approaching a hostile alien craft. Impact at current velocity will occur in six point two seconds."

It's not just any hostile sector, either. I've stumbled into the Stricker Quadrant, the most dangerous neighborhood in the known universe. I should have been paying closer attention. That'll teach me to eat chips and salsa while I'm jetting at 1.843 times the speed of light.

With a flick of my thumb, I reverse all thrusters. I cut the engines as fast as I can. But it's not fast enough. All it does is slow me down just before—*SKRA-PLAM!*—I crash straight into the mother of all mother ships.

I'm dazed. I'm confused. I try to scramble into my survival pod so I can jettison myself to safety, but there's no time for that. A huge robotic claw sweeps out from the side of the mother ship and pries open my cruiser like a can of tuna fish.

"WHAT IN THE WORLD DO YOU THINK YOU'RE DOING?" a voice booms out, as the claw

reaches again and grabs me by the collar of my
space suit.

And that's when I know for sure that I've just
flown my last mission.

CHAPTER 4

DEALER'S CHOICE

Rafe? I asked you a question! What in the world do you think you're doing?!"

I shook my head to clear my thoughts. I blinked a couple of times.

And I realized, of course, that I wasn't in the outer reaches of space. It was just an out-of-the-way hallway at my school.

And I hadn't been piloting a spaceship at all. It was just my new skateboard. I'd been itching *all day* to try it out on the super-smooth hallways after school let out.

And even though I hadn't just been nabbed by a hostile alien species, I *was* in danger. Big-time. Because I'd just crashed my board right into the last person on earth you'd want to do that to.

Also known as my principal, Mrs. Stricker.

"On second thought," Mrs. Stricker said, "I don't *care* what you think you're doing. Just march!"

Less than a minute later, I was back in the principal's office—again—and waiting for my latest punishment—again.

I don't want to brag, but if Hills Village Middle School had a Detention Hall of Fame, they'd practically have to name it after me. So I was pretty sure about what was coming next.

But I was wrong, wrong, wrong.

"Rafe, today just might be your lucky day," Mrs. Stricker told me. "Normally, I'd give you at least five detentions for a stunt like that. However, I want to offer you a deal."

"Excuse me?" I said.

The thing is, Mrs. Stricker doesn't *do* deals. Not unless "buy one detention, get ten free" counts. "It sounded like you just said you wanted to offer me a deal," I told her. "But that can't be right."

"You heard me correctly," Mrs. Stricker said. "We're in a rare moment where you actually might be of assistance to me, for once in your life. Extraordinary, I know. Here is your choice: you can either report to detention every Tuesday for the next five weeks, or—"

"I'll take the other thing," I said.

It didn't matter what it was. If I got another month's worth of detention, my brain was going to shrivel up and die of boredom. Seriously.

"Very well," she said, and got up to go. "Follow me."

"Where are we going?" I asked.

"Across the street to the elementary school," she said. And I thought, *Did I just get myself sent back to fifth grade?* Maybe Mrs. Stricker was so sick of me, she was sending me back to my old school.

But it wasn't that, either.

"Mrs. Melindez broke her leg slipping on a ketchup spill in the cafeteria today," Mrs. Stricker said. "I've been asked to find a substitute teacher for the after-school art program. That's going to be you."

"Seriously?" I said. "I can't believe you want me to teach *anything*."

"I don't," she said. "But I am in a bit of a pinch at this late hour."

"Wow," I said. "That must be *some* pinch!"

I mean, I know something about art. It's my best subject in school. Actually, it's my only good subject in school. But still, I'm about as far from being a *teacher* as you can get. I'm more like the kid who makes teachers wish they'd chosen some other profession.

Not that I was arguing. I mean, one hour of teaching art to little kids, in exchange for five hours of detention? That *was* a good deal.

Besides, it was too late to turn back now.

Operation: Nuclear Sub(stitute Teacher) was under way.

CHAPTER 5

ROUGH LANDING

 **Y**ou will stick to the basics. Paint, drawing, or clay," Mrs. Stricker said while we walked, double time, over to the elementary school. "You will give the students an assignment they can take home at the end of the hour. And you will behave responsibly, or you *will* be sent back to detention. Have you got that?"

"Got it," I said.

"Good, because here we are," she said.

We were standing outside a closed classroom door now. On the other side, it sounded like someone was moving furniture. And breaking things.

And I heard yelling, too. Lots and lots of yelling.

"What's all that noise?" I asked.

"That," she told me, "is your class."

"But how—"

"Good luck," she said. I had a feeling the rest of that sentence was something like "because you're going to need it." But Mrs. Stricker didn't stick around long enough for me to find out.

So I reached out, opened the art-room door, and—

FWOOM!

It was like getting punched in the face. By a tornado. Made of third graders.

"Okay, you guys!" I called out. "Everyone come over here, sit down, and listen up."

I'll give you four guesses for what happened after that:

(A) Everyone came over here

(B) Everyone sat down

(C) Everyone listened up

(D) None of the above

If you guessed (D), you win. Meanwhile, I hadn't even started and I was already losing. I could just smell those detentions getting closer.

So what do I do next? I move on to Plan B, of course. I reach out and push the big red button on the wall. The one marked SCHOOL-BOT 2000 AUTOMATED SYSTEM. USE ONLY IN EMERGENCIES.

Then I let the automated system do the rest.

A secret panel slides open in the ceiling. Twelve metal Frisbees with embedded homing devices fly out and hover in the air next to me, waiting for their next command.

"Fetch!" I tell them. And just like that, they

move in on their targets, each one attaching itself to the butt of a different kid.

"SYSTEM ENGAGED!" the system tells me. Which means I'm ready for Plan B, Phase Two.

"What's going on?" a little kid asks.

"I can't get this thing off me!" another says.

"Proceed to Phase Two!" I tell the system.

A loud humming noise fills the air as the electric magnets in the art-room seats buzz to life.

"Hey!" another kid says, as he's pulled across the room by the back of his pants.

"What's happening?" another asks, just before—*CLUNK!*—his metallized rear end attaches to the magnets in his chair. Followed by eleven others.

CLUMP!

CLANK!

CLOMP!

BUMP!

ZZT!

BANG!

FWIP!

SHLIP!

BLORNG!

FWANK!

TRANK!

And just like that, I've taken control of my class. Not bad for a first-time substitute, huh?

The only problem being, of course, that I wasn't so lucky. But you already knew that, didn't you?

In fact, I was still just standing there, wondering how to get twelve little kids to sit down, make some art, and keep me from landing in middle-school prison every Tuesday for the next five weeks. Which meant it was time for the *real* Plan B.

So I did what older brothers have done for all of eternity, whenever they need to get something done.

"HEY!" I yelled in my big-brother-est voice. "EVERYONE PIPE DOWN AND FIND A SEAT OR I'M NOT GOING TO BE HELD RESPONSIBLE FOR WHAT HAPPENS NEXT!"

That used to work on my little sister, Georgia, every time. It doesn't anymore, but it sure got these kids' attention. They all stopped and stared at me like I actually meant what I said. And after that, everything went just *great*.

For about another twenty seconds.

CHAPTER 6

LET'S TRY THAT AGAIN

 **N**ow that I had their attention, I passed out paper, paints, and paintbrushes to get the kids going. Maybe this wasn't going to be so hard after all.

"Okay, guys, here's what you're going to do," I said. "I want you to paint a picture of your house."

"That's SO boring!" one kid said.

"I hate painting!" another kid said.

"Can I paint something else?" someone asked.

"No," I said. "That's the assignment, and that's that."

I really did sound like a teacher now, which was kind of depressing. But I couldn't afford to mess around.

"Any questions?" I asked, and one girl's hand shot up. "What's your name?"

"Melinda," she said.

"Thanks for raising your hand, Melinda," I said. "And what's your question?"

"Where's Jake?" she asked.

"Who?" I asked.

"Jake," another kid said. "You know. *Jake.*"

I still didn't know which one was Jake, so I did a quick head count of my twelve students and came up with...eleven heads.

"Did anyone see Jake?" I asked, and all eleven hands went up. "Great! And who saw where he went?" All eleven hands went back down.

Oh, man! I didn't know how many detentions I might get for losing an actual kid, but something told me it was more than five.

Okay, Khatchadorian, I thought. *Don't panic. You've got this.*

"Everyone just wait here," I said. Right before I realized that probably wasn't a good idea.

"Actually, everyone come with me," I said. Right before I realized that wasn't such a good idea, either. The second we left that room, all eleven of them were going to spin off in eleven different directions.

So I thought of something else.

"Change of plans," I said. "Everyone give me your shoelaces."

"What for?" Melinda asked.

"The faster you give me your shoelaces, the sooner you'll find out," I said.

It took a few more minutes after that, but pretty soon, I was ready to go.

"All right, people, let's move out," I told them. "Keep your eyes peeled and your minds sharp. Operation: Find Jake At All Costs is a go!"

CHAPTER 7

HiDE AND SEEK
(AND SEEK, AND SEEK)

We turned that school upside down. We went up the hall, shouting for Jake and looking in every open room. We checked the boys' bathrooms. We checked the girls' bathrooms. We checked the music room, the auditorium, the gym, the locker rooms, and the underside of all the buses in the parking lot.

No Jake.

Nope. Not under here, either.

By the time we headed back to the art room, it was 4:15 and I had exactly fifteen minutes to find Jake and get the kids to make some art before the parents showed up. Either that, or leave town and never show my face in Hills Village again.

But then it turned out that I didn't have to decide. Because when we got back, there was Jake, sitting at one of the tables.

"Where have you guys been?" he asked.

"Where have *we* been?" I asked. *"Where were you?"*

He pointed down, under his table. "Taking a nap," he said. "We had subtraction today, and math makes me really sleepy."

And while I could relate to the math part, I didn't have time to be mad. I now had *fourteen* minutes left, and the kids were already getting crazy again. I had to yank one of them off the windowsill just before she could climb outside.

And that's when it hit me. These kids were like twelve of *me*. Twelve little Rafes, running around like crazy, getting into trouble, and just about impossible to focus.

So I needed something to get their attention.

Something that would have gotten *my* attention when I was their age.

And then my brain went *STORM!* And I knew what we were going to do.

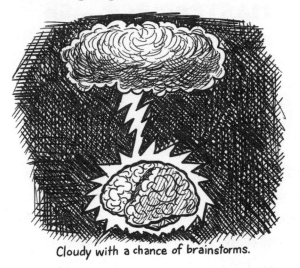

Cloudy with a chance of brainstorms.

"Okay, guys," I told them. "We don't have much time, so I have a new idea. I want you all to paint me instead."

"BORING!" said the same kid as the last time.

"That's even more boring than painting a house!" Melinda said.

"No, it's not," I said. "See, I don't think you're getting my drift. Let me try that again...."

CHAPTER 8

MASTERPIECE...iSH

 **F**or the rest of the hour, the kids *really* got into the assignment. I didn't have to *make* them do anything at all. They tackled this one like it was chocolate cake.

By the time the parents got there, our group project was done. It was a masterpiece! Well, close enough, anyway.

And all the kids wanted to get their picture taken next to their new creation so they could print out the photo at home and put it up on their refrigerators.

Because they'd done exactly what I'd told them to do.

They'd painted *me*.

When Mrs. Stricker came in to see how
everything had gone, she looked like she was going
to self-destruct.

"What in the WORLD...?" she started to say,
just before Melinda's mom interrupted.

"Mrs. Stricker, I don't know what you told this
young man, but I've never seen my daughter more
excited about art!!" she said. "I certainly hope he'll
be teaching the rest of your art program!"

The other kids were nodding. The parents were
smiling. And Mrs. Stricker looked like Melinda's
mom had just been speaking Martian.

"I, uh…well…uh…." she said. "The original teacher *is* going to be out for a while with a broken leg. So…I suppose that's up to Rafe."

And since something told me I was going to need to cash in some of my other detentions (the ones I hadn't gotten yet), and also because I ended up having a blast with those crazy kids (believe it or not), I said that sounded like a good idea to me.

So who knows? Maybe I have a whole career as an art teacher ahead of me. Or maybe I just got lucky that day. All I know for sure is that sometimes, a little imagination can go a long way.

And a lot of imagination can go even further.

CHAPTER 9

ONE STEP FORWARD,
ONE VERY BIG STEP BACK

 **A**s soon as Rafe was done on stage, I came out to introduce our first musical guest—Maroon 5, who started rocking the house while the audience went wild. (I told you it was going to be a big show!)

Right after that, I heard Storm Kidd's voice over my headset.

"Okay, everyone, we have four minutes until our next storyteller, Bick Kidd. Would Bick Kidd please report to the stage? Bick Kidd to the stage, please."

"You can just call me Bick," he radioed back. "I am your brother, after all."

"Less talking, more walking, little brother," Storm said. "You're up next."

As for Storm, I couldn't think of a better

person to have as our stage manager on this monster show. Broadcasting to millions of people meant keeping track of millions of details, and if Storm were a computer, she'd be the kind with an eighteen-terabyte brain.

So everything was going great, right?

Well, yes and no.

"Jimmy," Storm said. "You have a visitor, and I think we have a little problem. By which I mean, I think we have a *big* problem."

When I got off stage, I saw a lady in a business suit waiting for me. I didn't know what she wanted, but that suit gave me a bad feeling. She looked like the only person for a mile around who wasn't there to have a good time.

"Hi, I'm Jimmy," I said. "Can I help you?"

"I certainly hope so," she said, and handed me her business card. "My name is Violet Bash, and I'm here from the Washington Association of Special Permits."

"The...W.A.S.P.?" I said.

Violet Bash

☎ (202) 357-2020
📱 (555) 555-4321
✉ VBash@wasp.com

Washington Association of Special Permits

"That's correct," she said. "I understand you've advertised this festival to run all day?"

"Yes, ma'am," I said. "We're just getting started. We're going to have stories on the main stage, open mic, music, and all kinds of other—"

"Doubtful," she said. "According to the paperwork you filed with our office, you're only permitted to use this space for another"—she stopped to look at her watch—"fifty-two minutes."

"WHAT?" I asked.

"See for yourself," she said, and stuck a copy of our permit into my hand.

Which is when I started to realize that I'd made a huge mistake.

Like, extra huge.

This event will run from:
11:00 AM ☑ PM ☐ to
12:00 AM ☐ PM ☑

Tiny check mark,
HUGE mistake.

Do you see where I checked off 12:00 p.m.? That was the problem. I'd intended to make sure we could use the National Mall for the entire day, until midnight. Which is 12:00 *a.m.*

Not 12:00 p.m.

Which meant that we were now less than an hour away from getting shut down like a water park with a shark sighting. All because I put that one little check mark in the wrong place!

"We have ten thousand people here," I told Mrs. Bash. "I can't just tell them to go home because of a dumb mistake I made. There has to be something I can do to fix this."

"The only possible solution is for you to file a new permit at the W.A.S.P. office across town," Mrs. Bash said. "But I'm afraid getting there and returning with the correct paperwork in time will be nearly impossible."

"Aha!" I said. "*Nearly* impossible, but not impossible."

"It's just a figure of speech," she said.

"*Or is it?*" I asked. But I didn't wait around for an answer, because there was only one way to find out, and the clock was already ticking.

I couldn't let this happen.

In fact, I *wouldn't* let it happen.

No way.

No how.

Not if I had anything to say about it.

CHAPTER 10

ON THE FLY

Jimmy, where are you?" Storm said over the headset. "I need you back on stage in thirty seconds to introduce Bick."

"Change of plans, Storm," I said. "Jacky? Jamie? Are you two on this frequency?"

"Ha-Ha here!" Jacky radioed back.

"Welcome to Taco Bell, may I take your order?" Jamie joked.

"I need you guys to step in for me as emcees," I told them, and explained everything as fast as I could.

Jacky's a real-life movie star, and Jamie is the world's best kid comic. If anyone could host this thing while I was gone, it was them.

"You want some company, Jimmy?" I heard Rafe

over the headset. "I just did my thing, so I'm free."

"That'd be awesome," I said. I figured some backup couldn't hurt.

Meanwhile, Storm just kept rolling with it like a well-greased tumbleweed.

"In that case, Jacky Hart, please report to the stage to introduce my brother Bick," Storm said. "After that, Michael Littlefield and David Scungili are up next and Jamie will introduce them. Rafe, you can meet Jimmy off stage left. Everyone copy?"

"Got it!"

"Copy!"

"No prob!"

"Hurry back, Jimmy and Rafe!"

Meanwhile, we had to get going. Every second counted now—otherwise, we risked getting the entire show shut down before we could make it back in time.

"Storm, can you call us an Uber?" I asked.

"Already done," she said. Because she's *that* good.

"I'm here!" Rafe said, coming up behind me. "Let's get this done!"

Then I turned to Mrs. Bash before I took off.

"Just promise me you won't shut down the show before I'm back," I asked.

"I can promise that I won't shut it down for"— Mrs. Bash looked at her watch again—"another forty-nine minutes. You'd best get moving."

So we started running like crazy to catch that Uber...

...to get to the W.A.S.P. office...

...to file the *correct* paperwork...

...to bring it back to Mrs. Bash...

...to keep this whole show from going down like the *Titanic.*

"We've got this," Rafe said as we piled into the car. "Jimmy and Rafe for the win!"

"It's not really a game," I said.

"We'll see about that," he said. Because if you know Rafe, he can turn pretty much anything into a game.

Anyway, I was glad he was along for the ride.

"How fast can you get us there?" I asked the Uber driver.

"I'll do my best," he said, and we took off. Lucky for me, he drove that car as if it were the *Millennium Falcon,* instead of just a Toyota Camry.

Once we were moving, I pulled out my phone so I could keep track of the live show while we were on the road. Jacky was already on stage and killing it. Now I just needed a giant dose of good luck to help me undo my own stupid mistake. Because the clock wasn't going to stop running for anyone.

And this was all on me.

But enough about me, folks. Let's bring our next storyteller to the stage. Hey, Bick Kidd! Get your treasure-hunting butt out here!

CHAPTER 11

BARGAIN BASEMENT

It all started when we went to help our Aunt DeeDee clean out her basement.

I know, that's probably not where you'd expect a treasure-hunting story to begin. But sometimes these things happen where you least expect.

The four of us—me, Tommy, Storm, and my twin sister, Beck—were all pretty bummed to be spending a nice Saturday morning in a dusty old basement. But we couldn't say no to our favorite aunt. She was getting older and couldn't afford to live in that big old house of hers anymore. So we said we'd come and help her pack.

"Hand me another box," Tommy said. "There are some books I want to clear off this top shelf."

Tommy's the tallest, so he was in charge of all the high-up stuff. One second, I heard him sweeping a bunch of books into the box I'd handed him, and the next second I heard *CLUNK!*

And then *"OW!"*

When I looked over, Tommy was rubbing his head. Next to him, a big leather-bound book lay on the floor.

"That thing is *heavy*!" he said.

Storm went to pick it up. "Wow, it really is!" she said. "What is this?"

It was the size of a little suitcase, with a faded gold monogram engraved onto the cover.

Who???

Real leather! They don't make them like this anymore.

"Who's GK?" I asked, just before we heard Aunt DeeDee on the stairs behind us.

"Oh my. Look what you kids found," she said. "This house is absolutely filled with memories. I sure am going to miss living here."

"Is the *K* for Kidd?" Storm asked.

"It sure is," DeeDee told us. "That journal belonged to your great-great-great-great-aunt Geraldine Kidd. She was one of the only lady gold prospectors in the nineteenth century."

"Cool!" Beck said.

"Some people say that the adventurous streak in our family was born with her," Aunt DeeDee added.

"She sounds awesome," Tommy said.

"Actually," DeeDee told us, "I'm afraid hers isn't a story with a happy ending."

"Mauled by bears?" I asked.

"Drowned in the Colorado River?" Tommy asked.

"Poisoned by a rival prospector?" Storm asked.

The truth is, my siblings and I came by our imaginations honestly. We've been all over the world, and we've seen some crazy things. They

don't call our family the Treasure Hunters for
nothing. Tommy even has fans—mostly the young,
female, scream-y kind.

"No, no, it was nothing like that," Aunt DeeDee
said. "Why don't you bring that journal upstairs,
and I'll tell you all about the true, sad story of
Geraldine Kidd."

CHAPTER 12

THE BALLAD
OF GERALDINE KIDD

Storm set Great-Great-Great-Great-Aunt Geraldine's journal on the dining room table with another *CLUNK!*

I leaned in for a closer look. I wasn't sure how interesting this was going to be, but pretty much anything was better than cleaning out that basement.

"The first hundred pages or so are fascinating," Aunt DeeDee told us. "But in the end, it all just turns to gibberish. The poor thing spent so much time alone, from Carlsbad Caverns to Tahiti and everywhere in between, I think she might have lost her mind along the way."

And Aunt DeeDee was right. The whole first part of that book was page after page of handwritten notes, all about the places Geraldine went and the treasures she found…or didn't find.

July 8, 1848:

Fine morning. New horse hitched up to the tackle without any problem. I'll be in Shasta, California, by Tuesday. Word is, there's a mountain of gold to be found up that way. Which is exactly what I intend to do.

August 14, 1848:

I'm sorely disappointed in Shasta, and also in myself. It's been eight days, and I've got nothing but dusty lungs to show for my labor.

August 31, 1848:

Oh my! Oh my! Oh my! I feared this day would never come, but come it has! I shan't say too much here. It's too dangerous, with too many prying eyes all about! But you know where to find me.

"'You know where to find me'?" Storm asked. "Who's she talking to?"

"Maybe us future Kidds," Beck said. "Her descendants."

"It's possible," Aunt DeeDee said. "That journal has been handed down from generation to generation. But we may never know what she meant. That's the last entry before it all turns to nonsense."

Storm flipped another page, and the only thing written there were numbers. Lots and lots of numbers.

92-41-3
88-34-2
52-69-7
21-82-5
33-71-1
92-41-2
88-34-4
52-67-6
21-28-7
38-77-8

32-42-9
34-24-7
51-68-3
22-88-1
77-29-7
92-99-8
62-43-2
52-47-8
21-91-7
35-71-1

"That's so weird," Beck said. "It all changes, just like that?"

Aunt DeeDee shrugged. "I'm afraid so," she said. "But enough with the sad tales. How about you four get back to work and I'll start cooking up a nice batch of—"

"Hang on," Storm said. She was still staring at the pages with all the numbers on them. "I'm not so sure this is just gibberish."

Usually, when Storm says she's not sure about something, it means she *knows* something. She definitely had our attention now.

"Go on," Tommy said.

"This looks a whole lot like a cipher to me," Storm said.

"No way!" I said.

"A *what*?" Aunt DeeDee said, but the rest of us were already drooling. For us, something like that is completely irresistible.

"A cipher is a kind of code," Storm explained. "You can use it to spell out a secret message, if you have the correct source text."

"What kind of source text?" DeeDee asked.

"Like this journal," Beck said, tapping the book

on the table. "I'll bet the answer is right here in front of us."

Storm pointed to the first numbers on Geraldine's list. "See here? It says eighteen, sixty-six, three. That means we go to page eighteen…"

She flipped to the front, then counted forward eighteen pages.

"…and down to the sixty-sixth word," she said, and counted off with her fingers until she got to the word *detrimental.*

"That's the clue?" DeeDee asked. *"Detrimental?"*

"Hang on," Storm said. "It's eighteen, sixty-six, *three.* Which means we want the third letter in the sixty-sixth word. Which is *t.*"

"So *t* is the first letter in the secret message," Tommy said. "Awesome!"

"Yeah, but there are pages and pages of those numbers," I said. "It's going to take forever to get through all that."

"If it was easy, someone would have done it by now," Storm said. "I'm starting to think Geraldine Kidd knew *exactly* what she was doing."

You could feel it. Everyone was getting excited now.

"Aunt DeeDee, do you know what this means?" Tommy asked.

"I don't have a clue," DeeDee said.

"If this cipher is worth what I'm guessing it's worth, then you won't have to sell your house after all," Storm said. Already, she had her get-down-to-business face on.

In fact, we all did. Because we're Kidds. And we know the sweet smell of treasure when we get a whiff of it.

CHAPTER 13

CRACKING THE CODE

It took Storm until after midnight to work through that cipher. Which unfortunately meant that Tommy, Beck, and I had plenty of time to keep cleaning Aunt DeeDee's basement.

But when Storm finally called out that she was done, we popped out of that cellar like fresh toast from the toaster.

Beck got there first, and when she saw what Storm had done, she didn't look too happy.

"Whaaaat?" she said. "Is this some kind of joke?"

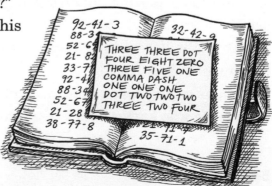

92-41-3
88-3
52-6
21-82
33-7
92-4
88-34
52-6
21-28
38-77-8

32-42-9

THREE THREE DOT
FOUR EIGHT ZERO
THREE FIVE ONE
COMMA DASH
ONE ONE ONE
DOT TWO TWO TWO
THREE TWO FOUR

35-71-1

"So maybe Geraldine was a little cuckoo after all," I said.

But Tommy was all over it. "Nope," he said. "Those aren't just numbers. They're coordinates."

Then he grabbed Storm's pen and wrote out the numbers another way.

Now I could see it. We're used to navigating around the globe, so longitude and latitude are our jam.

33.480351, −111.222324.

"Where do those coordinates point?" Beck asked.

"Right here," Storm said. She already had a map pulled up on her phone. "The Superstition Mountains in Arizona."

"Seriously?" Tommy said.

It felt like a cold breeze had just blown in from outside.

"Do you mean...*the* Superstition Mountains?" I asked.

"As in, the Bermuda Triangle of the American Southwest?" Beck asked.

"That's exactly what I mean," Storm said.

Anyone who knows about treasure hunting

knows that the Superstition Mountains are famous for two things: hidden gold and mysterious disappearances. People have been searching for the famous Lost Dutchman's Gold Mine up there for more than a hundred years. And a whole lot of the people who went looking were never heard from again.

"But if Geraldine knew where the gold was, why didn't she stake a claim?" I asked. "Why just write down the location?"

"One way to find out," Storm said. Already, her thumbs were tap-dancing through one of the travel apps on her phone.

In other words: next stop, Arizona. Because the Superstition Mountains may be dangerous, and mysterious, and no place at all for kids.

But they were *definitely* a place for Kidds.

Dear Aunt DeeDee:
Be back in a few days. Hopefully with good news!
xoxo,
T, S, B & B

CHAPTER 14

ROLF, MATILDA, CELINE, AND KLAUS

 **S**ixteen hours later, we landed in Phoenix and hired a driver to get us as far as Apache Junction. From there, we caught a ride with some hikers to the gear store near the Rogers Trough trailhead, in the foothills of the Superstition Mountains.

Geraldine's journal was too heavy to lug all the way to Arizona, but that was no problem. All we needed were those coordinates and Storm's photographic memory. Her brain would take care of the rest.

Now it was time to gear up and go.

At the store, we stocked up with a couple shovels, pickaxes, some rope, and plenty of water.

"You're going to want a satellite-based GPS

tracker, too," the lady behind the counter told us helpfully. Her nametag said HI! I'M LYDIA.

"It's okay," Beck said, holding up her phone. "I've got GPS right here."

"Trust me," the lady said, taking out a handheld unit for us. "You can't depend on your phone up in those mountains."

"She's right, Beck," I said. "Remember last year in Brazil?"

"Good point," Beck said. She took the locator from the lady and handed it over to Storm, who usually navigates for us anyway. "So, I guess we'll just be on our way—"

"Hey! I recognize you people," someone growled while we were waiting to sign out our stuff.

When I turned around, there was a man staring at me with his single good eye. The other eye was covered with a black lens in his glasses, like some kind of modern-day pirate. And why did I think that the shotgun over his shoulder had something to do with that missing eye?

"We get a lot of folks sniffing for gold around here," the guy went on. "And you're that treasure-hunting family, am I right?"

"Sheriff, you leave those kids alone," Lydia scolded. "They're just here for the hiking."

"Yeah, and I'm here for the waterskiing lessons," the guy said. Or rather, the sheriff said. I hadn't even noticed the badge on his overalls until now.

"Sir, I'm afraid you're mistaken," Tommy said. "We're the Bittendorffs. Rolf, Matilda, Celine, and Klaus."

That's our usual cover story, especially when we're on the trail of something good. Otherwise, we just end up with a lot of people tracking us while we're tracking the treasure. Maybe it wasn't a great idea to lie to a law enforcement officer like that. But then again, this sheriff looked like bad news.

"I'm just watching out for you Kidds," he said. "It can get mighty dangerous up there. Especially if people think you're here for a reason. A shiny reason that's worth a lot of pesos!"

But Tommy wasn't backing down. "I'm afraid you're mistaken, sir," he said again. "Like I already told you, we're the Bittendorffs—"

That's when someone else screamed. Really loud.

"AIEEEEE!!!! It's Tommy Kidd! I can't believe it!"

I couldn't believe it, either. Now we had three girls closing in on my brother, fast.

"You're just as cute in person!"

"I *live* for your Instagram!"

"Will you sign my backpack?"

People were *really* starting to stare.

"Bittendorff, huh?" the sheriff asked.

So much for our cover. It was feeling way past time to get out of there.

"We'll just take our stuff and go," I told Lydia, and she motioned me closer while Beck packed up, Storm put our coordinates into the GPS, and Tommy dealt with his fans.

"You kids watch your backs up there," she whispered. "Sheriff Rasher may wear that tin star of his, but he's greedier than a hungry mouse in a cheese factory."

"Really?" I asked. "The sheriff?"

"You betcha," she said. "I'm guessing he's going to try to follow you, and I suggest you shake him off quickly. I mean, assuming he's right and you're not just here for the hiking."

Then she smiled and winked. I winked back, without admitting anything. But I think we understood each other. The best thing now was to move out as quickly as possible.

"Come on," I said as I passed by my brother and his groupies. "It's time to hit the trail."

CHAPTER 15

SHAKING THE TAIL

 **B**y the time we reached the official trailhead, we had a whole posse of people pretending *not* to follow us.

Every time I looked back, another one of them was ducking behind a cactus, or stopping to tie their shoes, or staring at the sky like they weren't just waiting to copy our next move.

The only one who *wasn't* pretending was Sheriff Rasher. He kept his distance but he also just kept on coming. It sent a shiver down my back, even though the temperature was climbing toward a hundred degrees.

"We'll ditch those tourists first chance we get," Tommy said.

"It's not them I'm worried about," I said, and

told my siblings all about what Lydia at the gear store had told me. "I think it's the sheriff we really need to keep an eye on."

"We should worry about all of the above, I think," Beck said. "They all look suspicious to me." Then she turned around and snapped a few pictures of the "scenery." But I knew she was really documenting everyone's faces, just in case.

"This way," Storm, said with an eye on our rented GPS locator. "This thing actually works pretty well. Looks like it's going to be steep up ahead, but it's only a couple of miles to Geraldine's hiding place."

We went as fast as we could, picking up five hundred feet of elevation in the first half hour. We crossed a couple of log bridges and went single file along the edge of a sheer cliff. Then through some scrub pine until we came to the mouth of a narrow, twisting canyon.

It was blazing hot under the burning sun, with no shade to hide from it. All of us had buckets of sweat pouring off us. A bunch of the people following us had dropped off by now, but we still had Sheriff Rasher on our tail.

"This is where we make our move," Tommy said. "As soon as we hit that canyon, we'll be out of sight for at least a minute. When I say *go,* we're going to climb straight up and out of there. Then *poof!* We disappear."

Sounds like a plan, I thought. But it was too hot to talk.

We hiked on a little farther, until the notched rocky walls of that canyon had swallowed us up on either side.

"Okay, *now!*" Tommy said.

I'm the best climber, and I led the way. Those canyon walls had plenty of handholds. It wasn't hard to scramble onto a ledge, then another, and another, with the others right behind me.

Within a minute, we were about twenty-five feet off the canyon floor and just a few more handholds away from the top.

Meanwhile, we could hear footsteps thudding down below, closer and closer.

"Come on!" Tommy whispered. He launched himself over the top edge, then turned around and helped pull the rest of us up. A few seconds later, we were out of sight—and just in time, too.

Narrow Canyon, Narrow Escape!

I looked down to see Sheriff Rasher running by, directly below us. We all stayed perfectly still, holding our breath until he'd moved through the little canyon and out of sight again.

Then we crawled away from that edge and kept on moving before he could figure out his mistake and come after us.

So far, so good. It was looking like we had some luck on our side that day.

But here's the thing about luck: It can change at any time.

And without warning.

CHAPTER 16

A SLIPPERY SLOPE

Which way from here?" Beck asked.

"Up, again." Storm pointed to the steep mountainside in front of us. "Just another half mile to go."

"Yeah, but what a half mile!" I said. This was going to be the hardest part, by far. At least we had the trail to ourselves now.

Where we needed to go.

45-degree angle!

Gallons of sweat.

Running out of water.

Fifty pounds of gear. Oof!

So we climbed and clawed and sweated our way up that slope. My feet slipped out from under me a bunch of times and I slid back more than once. Geraldine Kidd had made good and sure that finding her secret place would be no picnic. But, hey, if we could use this treasure to help Aunt DeeDee pay off her house, it would all be worth it.

And then finally—finally!—Storm gasped out, "This is it! We're here!"

"We are?" Beck panted back. "But there's nothing to see."

The only things around us were more gravel, more rock formations, a few cacti, and some extra-large boulders, baking in the sun.

Storm watched the locator in her hand and took a few more steps over. "According to our coordinates, we need to be right…" She clapped her hand down on a rock that was as tall as she was. "…here!"

For a second, nobody said anything. We were all figuring it out at the same time. I could see it in the others' eyes.

Because—duh—buried treasure tends to be exactly that. *Buried.*

"How do we get under this boulder?" Tommy said. "Come help me move it!"

We all got uphill of that massive rock and started heaving. It wasn't easy. We pushed as hard as we could, and still, that boulder budged only a tiny fraction of an inch.

"Again! Heave!" Tommy said.

This time, it budged *two* fractions of an inch, but fell right back into place before we could really make any progress.

"Harder!" Beck yelled. "Don't quit now!"

We pushed with everything we had, and the rock tilted more than ever. It was *so* close to rolling away, but not close enough. This time, it landed back in its spot with a huge *WHOMP!* that shook the ground under my feet. I felt the vibration all the way up my legs.

"Oh, man!" Tommy wiped away more sweat. "Any other ideas?"

But I wasn't paying attention to Tommy now.

"What's that noise?" I asked.

"What noise?" Storm said, as a thin trickle of gravel started running past our feet.

"Shh!"

Everyone went quiet. The sound was like a low rumble of thunder in the distance. Except it was also coming closer. Quickly.

"LOOK!" Beck said. Her hand shot out and pointed straight uphill.

And that's when we all saw it. A massive landslide of rock, gravel, and more boulders the size of Volkswagens was flowing right down the mountain.

And it was heading straight for us.

CHAPTER 17

THE UNDERNEATH

 **W**e scattered like cockroaches.
Boulders went tumbling past. One of
them nearly mowed me down like a
speeding bus, but I dove just in time.
Tommy grabbed Storm and pulled her out of the
path of another one. Beck ran off to the side faster
than any of us, because she's smart that way.

Dust filled the air, and the rumbling sound
filled my ears. I could feel it vibrating the whole
mountainside for a long time.

And then, just as suddenly, it was over. The
sun beat down on my back where I'd landed. I sat
up, coughing out dirt and looking around for my
family.

When I got up, a whole layer of gravel and more

dust poured off me. But I was in one piece, anyway. We all were.

"Everyone okay?" Tommy asked.

Beck spit hard. "Yuck! I hate the taste of dirt!"

"I'm okay," Storm said. "But I think maybe the Superstition Mountains are fighting back."

"Or maybe that was Geraldine Kidd's booby trap," Beck said.

"*Or,*" Tommy said, "we figured out her trick for getting rid of that boulder."

When he pointed at the spot where that boulder had been, the only thing there now was a black hole in the ground.

"Yes!" Beck said. She threw herself down and shined her flashlight into the hole. "You guys!" she said from inside. "There's a cave down here!"

"Well, what are we waiting for?" Tommy asked.

We secured a rope to a cactus and lowered ourselves into the hole, one by one.

"What is this place?" I asked, when my feet hit the stone floor.

"Do you think it's the Lost Dutchman's Gold Mine?" Beck asked.

"Seems too small for that," Storm said.

She was right. It wasn't much of a cave at all. More like a little stone room.

But it wasn't completely empty, either.

"Hey! Check it out!" Tommy said.

I spun around and looked where his flashlight was pointing. And there, tucked into a tiny alcove in the rock, was an old wooden chest. It was chained right to the wall with a rusty padlock on the front.

That wasn't all. Right there on the chest's lid, we could just make out a faded gold monogram.

It said *GK*.

"We did it, you guys!" Storm said. "We really did it!"

"It's almost too easy. What's the catch?" Tommy asked.

And that's when we heard the unmistakable cocking of a shotgun behind us.

CHAPTER 18

OPEN AND SHUT CASE

 **D**on't move a muscle, kids," a voice came from overhead. "Or maybe I should say, *Bittendorffs*."

I recognized that voice right away. And it wasn't Sheriff Rasher's.

Nope. It was Lydia from the gear store.

"Don't shoot!" Storm said, and we put our hands up. "It's us, Lydia!"

But the voice just laughed, and not in a good way. That's when I started to realize that nothing—and no one—in the Superstition Mountains was really how it seemed.

In other words, Lydia wasn't there for the scenery, and she wasn't there to congratulate us on our big find, either.

"How did she find us?" Tommy said under his breath.

"You kids are even stupider than I thought," Lydia said. Then she held up a GPS locator, just like the one we'd rented from her. "You'd be surprised how easy it is to put a tracker inside a tracker. Then all I had to do was wait for you to ditch that idiot Rasher and follow your signal up here. From a distance, of course."

"You told me to watch out for the sheriff," I said.

So I guess Rasher really had been looking out for our safety the whole time.

"I told you to *ditch* the sheriff," she corrected me. "In fact, you did him a favor. I'd have had to shoot him dead if he'd gotten in the way. There's not enough room up on this mountain for him and me both."

"Technically," Storm said, "that's not true—"

"Shut up!" Lydia said, and raised her shotgun again. "I haven't been slaving in that dirty old gear store all these years for nothing. Now, I want you to pass up that chest, nice and easy. Or else," she warned.

"It's chained to the wall," Tommy said. "How are we supposed to—"

BLAM!

The sound of a shotgun blast filled that little cavern and just about exploded my eardrums. So I guess Lydia wasn't bluffing.

She had good aim, too. When I looked back, that old padlock was blown to smithereens and the chain had fallen away.

"Let's try that again," Lydia told us. "Hand over the loot."

It wasn't like we had much choice. We were cornered.

Tommy put a hand on either side of the chest and yanked it out of its little alcove. But when he turned to face the rest of us, he stopped.

"What's the problem, kid?" Lydia asked.

"It's too light," Tommy said. He shook the chest like a Christmas present, and there was no noise from the inside. Then he flipped the whole thing over and let the lid flop open. "See? It's empty."

"What the…" Lydia said. She shined her light down at us again, and Tommy held the chest up to show her. Sure enough, there was nothing in there.

"Hold that thought," Lydia told us. "And don't go anywhere."

"Very funny," Beck said.

For a long time, nothing happened. I heard Lydia muttering to herself, including a couple of words you don't hear in PG movies. Then finally, she stepped back into view.

"Here's how it's gonna go," she told us. "You can't prove a thing, and for that matter, I didn't take anything from you, seeing as how there's nothing to take. So you four are going to sit tight in that hidey-hole down there until morning. If I catch you behind me on the trail, I might just 'mistake' one of you for a cougar and put a bullet in you. Got it?"

"Whatever," I grumbled.

"Understood," Tommy answered for us.

So we stayed put with that empty chest while the lamest bandit in Arizona took off without us— and without any treasure.

CHAPTER 19

NOTHING AS IT SEEMS

 **W**hat a colossal waste of time," I said.

"Well, not necessarily," Storm answered.

"What are you talking about?" Tommy asked. "We've got nothing to show for all this trouble except a long, cold night in a small cave."

"Guess again," Storm said. Then she took Tommy's flashlight and shined it inside the chest. "Have a closer look."

We all gathered around, and our jaws dropped, one by one. Not because some kind of treasure had magically appeared. But because that chest wasn't quite as empty as I'd thought.

When I looked closely in the light, I saw what Storm had already noticed. There were numbers carved into the wood. Lots and lots of numbers.

"Is that
another cipher?"
Beck asked.

"Sure looks
that way," Storm
said. "Now
we just have
to get back to
Geraldine's
journal and figure out what it says."

"Wow!" Tommy said. "Didn't see that one
coming."

"Neither did Lydia," Beck said with a smile.

And in fact, the surprises weren't over yet.

I'm not going to say it was a pleasant night we
spent in that cave, but I've had worse. At least we
had something to look forward to.

Just after the sun came up, we climbed out of
there and headed down the mountain with that
"empty" chest strapped to Tommy's back.

When we reached the gear store at the
trailhead, it was all weirdly like it had been the
day before. There was Sheriff Rasher, hanging
out on the front porch. And inside, it looked like

business as usual, with Lydia still behind the counter.

"Excuse me, Sheriff?" Tommy said. "I think you need to arrest Lydia in there for threatening us."

"That so?" he asked, giving us a weird look. "Not sure what I owe you kids after I tried to watch out for you yesterday."

"And we're sorry about that," Beck said. "But—"

"Well, well, look who it is," Lydia said, coming out onto the porch. "When y'all didn't come down off the mountain last night, we figured you might have become four of its latest victims."

"Very funny," Storm said.

"We're fine," I told her. "No thanks to you."

The sheriff stood up then and faced her. "These kids are leveling some charges at you, Lydia. And I'm starting to wonder if you really went to visit your sick aunt when you closed up early yesterday."

"Of course I did!" she snapped. "Who're you gonna believe? Me, or these kids who ditched you on the trail when you were just trying to look out for them?"

Behind Sheriff Rasher's back, she gave us an evil eye. But I wasn't too worried.

"By the way, here's the GPS locator we rented from you," Storm said, and put it down on the porch with the rest of our gear.

"And you know, you were right," Beck said, holding up her phone. "We didn't get much signal up there at all."

"Of course you didn't," she said.

"But that's the thing about phones," Beck went on. "You don't need cell service to take photos and videos."

For a second nobody said anything. Then Beck turned her phone screen where Sheriff Rasher could see it, and she hit Play. It was all cued up.

"I told you to *ditch* the sheriff," Lydia's voice played out on the recording. "In fact, you did him a favor. I'd have had to shoot him dead if he'd gotten in the way...."

There was more, of course. A lot more. Because I don't have just one genius sister. I have two. And Beck had been smart enough to record the entire thing.

Five minutes later, Lydia was wearing some shiny new bracelets, also known as handcuffs, and going for a ride in the back of Sheriff Rasher's car.

Something told me the gear store was going to be looking for a new manager ASAP.

As for us, we'd done what we'd come to do. It was time to go home.

CHAPTER 20

HOME $WEET HOME

 **A** day and a half later, we were back at Aunt DeeDee's. The movers were coming the next day, and if we were going to get anything out of this treasure hunt, now was the time.

Storm set up at the dining room table with our new treasure chest and Geraldine Kidd's journal, while DeeDee put the rest of us back to work, cleaning the garage this time.

But finally, Storm called out for us to come have a look.

"You guys! Come in here, *right now*!" she said, and we thundered into the dining room like a small herd of cattle.

"What is it?" I asked. "What does the cipher say?"

The dining room table had something weird all

over it. Something that looked like…animal skin?

And in fact, it kind of was. Or at least, it had been. Now it was just strips of old leather that Storm had peeled away from the cover of Geraldine's journal.

Which is where it got interesting. Because now, the journal really did provide us with the answer to everything.

"Is that book cover made of…*gold*?" Beck asked.

"Sure looks that way," Tommy said.

"No wonder it was so heavy," I said. "Geraldine didn't just hide her treasure. She made her journal out of it."

Congratulations. You've proven yourself worthy of the Kidd name. Now skin this journal like a wild hare and claim your reward!

We ran to the bathroom scale next and determined that the journal had been made from a full twenty pounds of solid gold.

Twenty pounds!!!

Storm already had her nose buried in her phone again, tapping away. "So, at today's market rate," she said, "that's three hundred eighty-nine thousand dollars. Give or take."

"Plenty to get this house paid off," Aunt DeeDee said.

"Plus maybe a little left over, to get someone else to finish cleaning it," I said.

And if that was our reward, on top of seeing our favorite aunt taken care of, I'd say we made out pretty well.

Really, there was just one question left. Where to now?

Because like I already told you, we're Kidds. And we're always ready for the next adventure.

CHAPTER 21

SLOW GOING

 **B**y the time Bick finished telling his story, I was starting to freak out in the backseat of that Uber with Rafe. We'd hit a bunch of traffic, and the car was moving about as fast as a turtle in a peanut butter pool.

Meanwhile, we had only forty-two minutes left. That wasn't much time to reach the permit office, fill out the right form, and get back to the National Mall before Mrs. Bash shut us down.

"Excuse me," Rafe said to the driver. "If I told you someone's life depended on it, would you be willing to drive on the sidewalk?"

The driver's eyes went wide. "Someone's life depends on it?" he asked.

Rafe looked at me. I shook my head no.

"Well, not exactly," Rafe said. "I just wondered what would happen if it did."

"Do you know how much farther it is?" I asked the driver.

"About another mile," the guy said. "When do you gotta be back there, anyway?"

I looked at my phone again.

"Forty-one minutes!" I said.

"In this traffic?" He shook his head. "You'd have a better chance running on foot."

I looked at Rafe. Rafe looked at me.

"Are you thinking what I'm thinking?" I asked.

"You mean, running across the roofs of all those cars ahead of us?" Rafe asked, and held up his hand for a high five. "I've always wanted to do that!"

"Close enough," I said. "But let's stick to the sidewalk."

A second later, we were out of that car.

"Thanksalotandhaveagoodday!" I yelled over my shoulder, and we started sprinting up Massachusetts Avenue.

I pulled out my phone as I ran. I didn't want to lose track of the live show, so I kept moving with one eye on Rafe, one eye on the sidewalk, and one eye on my phone screen. (Or something like that. You get the idea.)

Back at the show, I saw Jamie Grimm was in the middle of introducing Michael and David for the next story. So at least everything was on track there. Now we just had to make sure it stayed that way.

CHAPTER 22

YOU'RE INVITED

**I** COULDN'T BELIEVE IT!

I mean, I *could* believe it, because it was right there in my hand—an invitation to the Cartoon Hall of Fame induction ceremony for Pottymouth and Stoopid. Those were the characters based on my best friend, Michael, and me. And it was happening at this year's Comic Con in New York City.

Yeah, *the* Comic Con.

In *the* New York City!

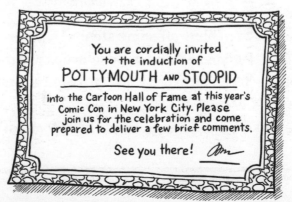

You are cordially invited
to the induction of
POTTYMOUTH AND STOOPID
into the Cartoon Hall of Fame at this year's
Comic Con in New York City. Please
join us for the celebration and come
prepared to deliver a few brief comments.

See you there!

The invite came in the mail, in a gold envelope and everything. So I wasn't dreaming. This was completely real. It was really happening.

"I can't believe it!" I said for about the ninetieth time, because...well...you know.

"David, please, *please* calm down," my mom said, like I was getting on her first and last nerves at the same time.

I couldn't blame her. I'd been bouncing around the house like a Ping-Pong ball for the past two hours, just waiting for Michael to get back from visiting his grandma so we could freak out about this together.

So far, I didn't even know if he knew about it yet. Or, if he did know about it, did he know that I knew about it too?

And did he know that I didn't know if he knew? I don't know! I was too busy freaking out on my own to figure it out.

"You need to blow off some steam," said my mom. "Go outside and shoot some hoops. Or run around the block once or twice. Or twenty times," she said.

I felt like I could run around the *moon* just

then, but I didn't have to. Because when I went outside, Michael's foster mother was just dropping him off in front of our house. And he was waving at me like crazy, with a bright gold envelope in his hand.

"And we have to give a speech?" Michael asked. "Like, a *real* speech?"

"That too," I said. "We need to come up with something really good to say."

"For sherkles," Michael said. He makes up a lot of his own words, if you didn't already know that about him.

And since the whole thing was just a week away, we decided to get right on it and start writing our speech ASAP.

You know. Just as soon as we were done freaking out.

Together!

CHAPTER 23

SPEECH-Y GOODNESS

 **A** week later, there we were, flying to New York City by ourselves. Someone from Comic Con was going to meet us at the airport, and it was the first time Michael and I had flown anywhere alone.

It was crazy. In a good way.

And you know what else was crazy? We hadn't gotten our speech figured out yet. Yeah, the same speech we swore we were going to start a week ago. How did *that* happen?

So we worked on it in the air, during the flight.

I didn't know how big the audience was going to be for this ceremony, but even if just one kid showed up, I was already super pumped about the whole thing. I felt about as excited as an overcaffeinated Chihuahua. Which is what I told Michael.

"That's what we should say at the ceremony!" he said.

"'Overcaffeinated Chihuahua'?" I asked.

"No," Michael said, and he started scribbling down some ideas. "Something like…'Even if only one kid likes what we did…'"

"Right!" I said. "Except we didn't actually do it, since someone else made those Pottymouth and Stoopid cartoons."

"Right," he said. "So…even if one kid likes what someone else did, but kind of did it because of us—"

"That's better," I said.

"—then everything we did, or didn't do, or *might* have done, even if we didn't know we were doing it...would all be worth it," Michael said.

"Makes sense to me!" I said. And we double high-fived up top and once down below. (That's our signature high five.)

"Also," I told Michael, "you should be the one to give the speech, not me. You're way better with words."

"Aw, fuzzlemush," Michael said. "Thanks, man."

CHAPTER 24

ON OUR OWN (IN A GOOD WAY)

 **W**hen we got off the plane, there was just one little problem with the person who was supposed to meet us at the airport.

There was no person to meet us at the airport.

People were coming and going everywhere, but none of them were holding a sign that said LITTLEFIELD AND SCUNGILI like I thought they were going to. Or even POTTYMOUTH AND STOOPID.

But who cares? We were in New York City! For Comic Con!

So we just started following the other people to see where the crowd took us, like a couple of trout floating downstream.

When we went outside, there were even more people.

"Hey, look!" Michael said.

Off to the right, there was a driver, in a dark suit, holding a sign that said LITTLEFIELD AND SCUNGILI, after all.

And right there, getting into the back seat of that car, were two guys who looked kind of like us, but...weren't us.

Before we could say anything, the limo with fake Michael and fake me took off, headed for the city. Or for somewhere, anyway. Just not with us inside.

"What the hicklesnicklepox?" Michael asked. "Those guys were impostors!"

But I was still too excited to worry. "It's kind of cool, when you think about it," I said. "How many kids do you know who have their own impostors?"

"Good point," Michael said. "But what should we do now?"

We *should* have called our parents.

We *should* have spoken to an adult who worked for the airport.

We *should* have made a careful decision and not done anything our folks wouldn't want us to do.

"Let's take a taxi into the city," I said.

"Works for me," Michael said.

And just like that, we had a new plan.

I had $40.00 on me, for food and stuff. Michael had $52.81, for a total of $92.81.

"That should be plenty," I said. "I mean, how much can one little taxi ride cost?"

FORTY-FIVE MINUTES LATER...

"That'll be ninety-eight dollars and fifty cents," the cab driver said when we pulled up in front of the convention center.

"Um..." I said.

"Uh..." Michael said.

"You've got to be kidding me," the driver said.

He ended up letting us give him our $92.81 plus

a free Pottymouth and Stoopid comic, which we would have signed for him, but he asked us not to.

But hey, who cares? Because we were finally here, at Comic Con! *The* Comic Con! And that convention center was off-the-hook amazing.

Not to mention, HUGE.

As soon as we got inside, I saw people in every kind of costume you can think of. It was like a whole comic book city, all under one roof.

"Was that…Scarlett Johansson?" Michael asked. And the thing was, it very possibly could have been.

There were people dressed as superheroes; megavillains; manga characters; anime characters; characters from Calvin and Hobbes, *Stranger Things, Star Trek, Star Wars,* and *Stargate;* and characters such as Star-Lord, Starfire, and Star-pretty-much-everything-else.

I saw Pikachu, the Incredibles, a bunch of Ghostbusters, Deadpool, Spider-Man, plus another Spider-Man, plus a whole bunch of other Spider-Men, plus a couple of dragon kings and a walking, talking poop emoji, too.

And that was all in the first five minutes! They

had everything here, everywhere you looked. The question was, where did we need to be for our big ceremony?

"Excuse me," I said to a half human, half tarantula who was walking by. "Do you know where the Cartoon Hall of Fame abduction—"

"Induction," Michael said.

"—induction…is?" I asked.

But when the guy pointed, all eight of his legs went in different directions. Before I could ask which leg was the right one, he was already scuttling off to somewhere else.

"Maybe there's an information booth around here," I said.

"Excuse me," Michael asked a lady dressed as Groot from *Guardians of the Galaxy,* "do you know if there's an information booth around here?"

"I am Groot," she said, and kept on moving.

So we decided to just try to find the ceremony ourselves. It had to be there somewhere, right? And we'd come this far on our own. It couldn't be *that* hard to find.

I mean, how big could that whole place possibly be?

CHAPTER 25

LOST

Finally, we found a directory to tell us where everything was.

And *that's* where we finally, finally found what we were looking for.

JATAWLI
ANIME SCREEN —— EAST FN 212 F
ROBOT DESIGN —— WEST 74 FQ 2
COSPLAY AWARDS —— EAST D 781
COMIC CREATION —— SOUTH 2D 47
ANIMÉ SCREENING — LEVEL 2 XM
BATTLE OF THE BANDS — LEVEL 3 XN
TOON CREATION —— MAIN 272 N
MEET AND GREET — A72 E F G
SIGNING —— H72
MEET-UP —— ABF
TALK —— 2/F
MEET —— 7
SALE —— R
SWAP —— 8
BATTLE —— 70
COSPLAY —— M421   7328
COLORING   ONTEST —— NORT   629
INKING   TRATION — WES
TOY DESI   ETITION — SO   OOR
2NFR

"There it is!" I said, pointing at one of the million things on that sign. "Cartoon Hall of Fame Induction Ceremony! East Building, South Wing, Fourth Floor, Hall C, Ballroom B."

"Got it!" Michael said, and turned to a passing Wonder Woman. "Excuse me, Mrs….um…Woman. Do you know where the East Building is?"

Lucky for us, she did. Once she pointed us in the right direction, we hiked about a mile through some long hallways, down two levels, back up one level, around a bunch of corners, and down an escalator, until we finally saw the right sign.

"East Building!" Michael said, and we high-fived, high-fived, low-fived right there on the spot.

As far as we could tell now, we were on the right track, but we still had to find the South Wing, Fourth Floor, Hall C, and Ballroom B.

So we just kept going. And that's when it all started getting a little weird. Kind of in a good way.

But also in a really…weird way.

CHAPTER 27

POTTYMOUTH AND STOOPID AND POTTYMOUTH AND STOOPID

 **A**s we walked into the next wing of the next hallway, things went from one kind of weird to another.

But a lot more familiar, too.

"Is it just me," I said, "or are there—"

"A whole lot of us here?" Michael said. "Yeah, it's not just you. I think we're getting closer."

We were definitely in the right neighborhood now. Because all of a sudden, everywhere I looked, it was like a river of Pottymouths and Stoopids. People were dressed up as them, and wearing masks of them, and sporting T-shirts with them on the front. It was amazing!

Not only that, there were a couple of Michaels and Davids, too! I didn't even know which ones were the impostors we'd seen at the airport and which ones were impostors of the impostors.

Then, as we came around the next corner, we saw the Best. Thing. Ever.

"Guh-wha?" Michael said. "I mean... fluffertastic!"

I'm not going to lie. My face turned kind of red, and my eyes maybe got a little wet. In a good way. I felt like we'd walked all the way to heaven. And then—

"Look!" Michael said, pointing at a big doorway with another sign over it. "Ballroom B: Cartoon Hall of Fame Induction Ceremony!"

We'd made it! We'd done it! All on our own!

And the next second, we were booking it right over to that ballroom.

"You have your speech notes?" I asked.

"Check!" Michael said.

"You ready to do this?" I asked.

"Check!" Michael said.

"Good thing," I said. "Because here…we…are!" I pulled open the door, and—

The place was empty.

"What the grizzlenoogie?" Michael said.

We'd found the right room, for sure. There was another whole Pottymouth and Stoopid banner on the wall. But there was also trash on the floor, and programs crumpled on the chairs, and a janitor sweeping the stage.

We were too late.

We'd missed it.

We'd missed the whole sludgepuggling thing, as Michael might say.

CHAPTER 28

JUST ONE

No way," Michael said.

"I can't believe it," I said. "After all that?"

I sat down in one of the thousand chairs in that place. It didn't matter which one. They were all empty.

"How could this happen?" Michael said. "We were supposed to—"

"Give a speech," I said. "And—"

"Everything," he said. "I know. And now—"

"We don't even have money for food," I said.

"That too," he said.

I felt like someone had blown my head up like a balloon and then let it fly all over the room until it landed all empty and shriveled on the floor.

Or something like that.

"What do we do now?" I asked.

And then a small voice came from the back of the hall.

"Did I miss it?" the voice said.

When we looked back, we saw a kid standing there. He was wearing a Pottymouth and Stoopid T-shirt. And he had a Pottymouth and Stoopid DVD in his hand. And a really, really sad look on his face.

"Yeah, sorry," I said. "We missed it too."

"Wait a second," the kid said. He started coming closer. "Are you them?"

"No," Michael said. "We're not Pottymouth and Stoopid. We're just—"

"No, I know," the kid said. "You're Michael and David. Aren't you?"

The way he said that, it sounded like being Michael and David was a *good* thing. Maybe even better than being Pottymouth and Stoopid.

Which was weird. But not in a bad way.

"Yeah, that's us," I said.

"NO WAY!" the kid said. "I've wanted to meet you guys since forever!"

Now it was my turn to say it.

"No way," I said.

"Way!" the kid said. "Can I get your autographs?"

And we signed his T-shirt, and his DVD, and his arm, right there on the spot.

"Sorry you missed the big ceremony," Michael said. "We did too. We were supposed to give a speech and everything."

The kid looked up at the stage, then back at us.

"Well, do you still want to give it?" he asked.

I looked at Michael, and Michael looked at me, and without saying a single word, we both knew exactly what our answer was. In a good way.

And I mean, in a really, really good way.

CHAPTER 29

THE NICK OF TIME

 **B**y the time Rafe and I finally stumbled into the W.A.S.P. office, I was up to about eighteen gallons. Of sweat. I'd never run that far, that fast, in that much heat, *ever*. I don't think Rafe had either. He was sweating even more than me.

I was losing time just trying to catch my breath and got about halfway through the reason I was there before the guy interrupted me.

"Ohhhh! You're Jimmy, aren't you?" he said. "We've been watching your show!"

He pointed at a TV set in the corner, where I could see the live show on the screen. Which was super cool, to know they were watching it.

"That's him, all right!" Rafe said, and slapped me on the back. "He's totally trending! So I'm not even exaggerating when I say that the entire country would appreciate it if there's anything you can do to help...."

I looked at Rafe now, trying to get him to tone it down a little. It was getting embarrassing.

"What?" Rafe whispered to me. "If you don't think big, you don't get anywhere."

And I couldn't argue with that. I *like* to think big. In fact, I like to think huge.

"Don't worry, kid. I think what you're doing is awesome," the guy said. "We'll have you out of here in a jiffy."

Sure enough, about two minutes later I had that new permit in hand, with the check marks in the right places and everything.

"Sweet!" Rafe said, and high-fived everyone around the office.

"What's the fastest way back to the National Mall?" I asked.

"And please don't say running!" Rafe added.

"You can hop the subway," the guy told us. "There's a Metro station right outside. Take the Red Line four stops to Judiciary Square. It'll be tight, but you should just make it."

"Red Line, four stops," Rafe said. "We've got this!"

Then we basically broke the sound barrier zooming out of that office building and down into the subway station.

"There's our train!" Rafe said. It was just pulling into the station when we got there. "Red Line, yes! Go, go, go, go!"

We hit the platform a second later, jumped on board, and fell into a couple of seats just before the train took off again.

Sweet!

When I checked the live show on my phone, Rihanna was out on stage, rocking the whole

National Mall. It still looked like everything was going well.

"Who's up after this?" Rafe asked.

"Your sister, Georgia," I told him.

"*That,* I don't need to see," he said. "Georgia's been practicing her story at home so much, even I know it by heart."

But at least we could relax, for a few minutes, anyway. In fact, all we had to do now was count four stops on the train and we'd be back where we'd started in no time.

Or at least, that's what I thought. See, we just assumed that we'd caught the *right* train going in the *right* direction.

Let's just say we were only *half* right about that.

CHAPTER 30

WHERE HAVE I HEARD THIS BEFORE?

 **O**nce upon a time, in the small town of Hills Village, there lived a girl named Georgia Khatchadorian (that's me!). She lived with her hardworking mother, Jules; her sweet grandmother, Dotty; and her devious, scheming, dreaming, walking disaster of an older brother, Rafe.

I know you've already met Rafe, but that was in his story. This one's mine, and I'll tell you right now—my brother is not the hero of this one. You'll see.

So anyway, it all started when our mother texted both of us at school one day.

Mom worked at Swifty's Diner, which served some of the best food this side of the planet. When I showed up after school, she handed me a huge bag of cheeseburgers, fries, and Swifty's signature apple pie.

"I want you to take this to your grandma, who is sick at the Woods'," Mom told me.

Burt and Marjorie Wood were Grandma Dotty's good friends, and she was house-sitting for them while they were on vacation. But now she'd come down with a bad cold and Mom said she could use some company.

"No sweat," I said. In fact, I was happy to do it, for two reasons.

One, I love hanging with Grandma Dotty. She's crazy, in a good way, and belongs in the Awesome Grandma Hall of Fame.

And two, I loved how jealous Rafe was going to be when he found out what he'd missed. My brother likes burgers and pie the way most people like water and oxygen.

"Stay warm out there, too," Mom said. "It's chilly today." She reached out and zipped my favorite red hoodie right up to my chin. "I want you to go straight to the Woods'. No stopping along the way, and no talking to strangers."

"Sure thing, Mom," I said, which was easier than telling her for the hundredth time that I'm not a little kid anymore. I can take care of myself. And besides, I really did plan on getting there ASAP. I mean, who likes cold cheeseburgers?

But you know what they say. Sometimes life gets in the way.

And other times, it's your devious, scheming, dreaming, walking disaster of an older brother who gets in the way.

This was one of *those* times.

CHAPTER 31

WHO'S AFRAID OF THE BIG BAD RAFE?

 **S**o there I was, taking a shortcut through City Hall Park on my way to the Woods', when I got blindsided by the Master of Disaster himself.

Also known as Rafe.

He came hurtling around the big fountain in the park, riding his skateboard and wearing his headphones, until—*SMASH!*—he plowed into me like a runaway train.

"RAFE!" I yelled. "Why don't you watch where you're going?"

He couldn't even hear me. He still had his stupid headphones on.

"I CAN'T HEAR YOU! I HAVE MY HEADPHONES ON!" he yelled.

(See?)

I pulled one earphone away and shouted, "I SAID...WATCH WHERE YOU'RE GOING!" Then I let it snap back into place.

"Ouch!" he said, and finally slid them off.

"Doing your homework, huh?" I asked.

"I'm just on my way to the library," he told me.

"Yeah, *right,* and I'm on my way to the Indy 500," I said. I *knew* the whole homework excuse had to have been fake. My brother is basically allergic to responsibility. I wouldn't trust him if my life depended on it.

But he wasn't listening anymore anyway. He was staring at that goodie bag in my hands. His eyes had gotten big, his nose was twitching, and if I wasn't mistaken, he was starting to drool.

"What's that?" he asked. "Do I smell apple pie? And...burgers?"

"It doesn't matter," I said. "It's not for you. It's for me and Grandma. She's sick at the Woods'."

"Well, hold on," Rafe told me. "You don't have to carry that big heavy bag all by yourself."

"Nice try," I told him, and started moving again.

"Hey, that's a really nice hoodie," Rafe said,

walking alongside me now. "Have I ever told you how nice you look in red?"

"And have I ever told you how obvious you are?" I said. "Buzz off, Rafe!"

"*Wait!*" he tried one more time. "Don't you think Grandma would like some flowers?" Then he pointed over at Frieda's Florist next to the park. "I bet you could get her something nice over there."

For once in his life, my brother had a good point. Grandma *loves* flowers. They'd make her feel even better than cheeseburgers.

"Yeah, okay," I said. "But you're chipping in too." I looked down to see how much money was in my pocket. "What kind of cash do you have on you?"

And the only answer I got that time was the sound of skateboard wheels rolling off into the distance. Which was absolutely typical. Whenever it's time to pay, all my brother wants to do is play.

But you know what? I didn't even care. At least it meant that Rafe was out of my hair for the rest of the day.

Or at least...that's what I thought.

CHAPTER 32

KNOCK, KNOCK! WHO'S THERE?

When I finally got to the Woods' house, the front door was locked, so I rang the bell.

"Who is it?" said a voice on the other side of the door.

It was a strange voice. A kind of Grandma-like voice.

But also, mostly…not.

"Hi, Grandma! It's Georgia," I called out. "I brought you a bag of goodies from Swifty's."

"Oh, dear," the voice said, followed by a bunch of fake coughing, with lots of fake phlegm mixed in. "I don't want to give you my germs, you sweet child. Just leave the food outside and I'll come get it once you're gone."

Oh, puh-leez!

"Grandma, what a deep voice you have!" I said. "It must be your cold."

"The better to keep you at a distance, my dear," answered "Grandma."

And by "Grandma," of course, I mean Rafe, who was just smart enough to think up a scheme like this, and just dumb enough to think I'd fall for it.

He hadn't even bothered to keep the real Grandma all the way out of sight. I could see her through one of the side windows, wearing Rafe's headphones and bopping on the couch to whatever music he had turned up loud for her.

Cough... cough... hack... hack...

Swifty's To Go

"Oh, and, Grandma," I said, "what big *lies* you have."

"Did you say *eyes,* dear?"

"Close enough!" I called through the door. "Well, okay, then. I'll just leave the food out here and be on my way. Bye, *Grandma!*"

But of course, I wasn't going anywhere. You already knew that, right?

See, I'd spent my life watching Rafe try to get away with one stupid thing after another, and I knew how his mind worked. Which also meant that I knew exactly what to do next. Or, as my brother might have put it—

Operation: SnareWolf was just about to begin.

CHAPTER 33

OPERATION: SNAREWOLF

 **I**f my mind worked the way Rafe's does, I'd probably imagine the next part to go something like this....

First, I pull out the decoy food bag that I brought with me. It's already stuffed with balled-up newspaper to look like a bag of cheeseburgers and pie. It's also loaded with an exploding ink packet, so when my brother opens it—*SPLURT!*—he'll be blue, literally, for the rest of the month.

Next, I set that decoy bag on the sidewalk. I put it just far enough from the door so that Rafe will have to come all the way outside to get it.

Then, while he's waiting inside for me to disappear up the street, I'm zipping around the side of the house. From there, I parkour up to the roof, tiptoe across to the chimney, and use my handy-dandy climbing rope to rappel inside, like I'm one-part ninja and one-part Santa.

By now, Rafe thinks I'm long gone. So while he starts sneaking out to pick up what he thinks is his next meal, I'm commando-crawling across the living room floor. I make my way to the front door, jump up, and—

SLAM! I close the door.

SPLURT! That ink packet goes off in Rafe's face.

CLICK! I've locked him out in the cold.

Which leaves my brother stuck outside with nothing but a bag of newspaper and a face full of ink to keep him warm, while Grandma and I settle in for the *real* feast.

And everyone lives happily ever after. Except for Rafe.

The end.

CHAPTER 34

LET'S TRY THAT AGAIN

Okay, yeah, I'll admit it. Something like that would be really cool. I mean, if it were even *possible*. That's where my brother falls short. His imagination always gets the best of him. Because whatever Rafe might *dream* about doing in fifteen complicated steps, I can actually get done in three easy ones.

Watch and learn.

STEP 1: CALL HIM OUT.

"Rafe, I know it's you!" I yelled from the front porch. "Just let me in."

"I can't heeeeeeear yooooooou," he called back, in that lame-o Grandma impersonation of his.

"If you open the door *right now*, I'll share all this food with you," I said. "But my offer is only good until I finish counting to three. Got it? One, two—"

Just like that, the door flew open faster than you can say...well...three. My brother has the worst case of BO I've ever seen. And by *BO*, I mean *Burger Obsession.* It was almost too easy.

"Why didn't you say that in the first place?" Rafe asked, like he hadn't been trying to scam me all along. "Come in, come in. Let's eat!"

STEP 2: PUT HIM OUT.

Meanwhile, Grandma was still jamming away with Rafe's headphones on. She didn't even know I was there yet, which was just how I wanted it for the time being.

"Oh, by the way," I told Rafe, "I bought some flowers like you suggested. Will you grab them off the porch while I get the plates and stuff?"

"Why'd you leave them outside?" he asked.

"To keep them fresh, of course," I said.

"They're right there," he said, pointing out the door. "Go get them yourself."

"Listen, do you want to eat or not?" I asked, holding the food bag just out of his reach.

And of course, that's all it took. Rafe practically

ran out the front door to grab those flowers.

Just before...

STEP 3: LOCK HIM OUT.

SLAM! I closed the door.

CLICK! I locked him out.

BAM! Mission accomplished.

And while Rafe pounded on the door to get back in, I waved over at Grandma to get her attention.

"HI, GRANDMA!" I shouted.

"HI, SWEETIE!" she yelled back. "RAFE TELLS ME I'M 'JAMMING' TO SOMETHING CALLED BRUNO JUPITER!"

"YOU MEAN MARS!" I shouted.

"WHAT?"

"NEVER MIND! YOU KEEP ON JAMMING!" I said. "I'LL BRING YOU SOME DINNER ON THE COUCH!"

Meanwhile, Rafe was still going. "GEORGIA! LET ME IN!" he yelled.

"YOUR BROTHER IS AROUND HERE SOMEWHERE," Grandma called out.

"HE HAD TO LEAVE SUDDENLY!" I told her.

"WHAT?" she asked.

"GEORGIA!" Rafe tried again. "LET ME IN, OR I'LL HUFF, AND I'LL PUFF—"

"Wrong story, loser!" I said through the door.

"I'M SO HAPPY TO HAVE *BOTH* OF YOU HERE!" Grandma went on. "HOW OFTEN DO I GET TO HAVE A DINNER DATE WITH MY FAVORITE GRANDCHILDREN?"

The truth is, Rafe and I are her *only* grandchildren, but I knew what she meant. And I almost wish she hadn't said that. Because sometimes making your sweet old grandmother happy is more important than anything. Even more important than taking revenge on your devious, scheming, dreaming, walking disaster of an older brother.

"Do I hear someone knocking at the door?" Grandma asked, finally slipping off those headphones.

Oh, well. I'd known it couldn't go on forever.

"It's just Rafe," I told her. "I guess he's back." Then I opened the door and he practically fell inside. "Way to go, Einstein," I said.

Rafe didn't even look at me. He walked straight

over to Grandma Dotty and handed her the bouquet that *I'd* bought at the flower shop.

"Here, Grandma. *We* bought you some flowers to make you feel better," he said.

"You two are spoiling me," she said. "What did I do to deserve such thoughtful grandchildren?"

"I don't know," Rafe said, giving her a kiss. "Just lucky, I guess."

And if you could have seen how Grandma Dotty's face lit up then, you would have kept your mouth shut about it too.

"Let's eat!" I said instead. Because that was the one thing we could *all* agree on.

So maybe it wasn't a happily-ever-after kind of situation, but I'll tell you this much: As we sat down to feast on that pile of food, I got a look from Rafe that told me he just might have learned a thing or two, or three, after all.

(1) I'm not a little kid anymore. Like I said before, I can take care of myself.

(2) Wolves are overrated.

And most important of all...

(3) Never, ever, ever mess with the girl in the red hood.

CHAPTER 35

MEANWHILE, SOMEWHERE IN WASHINGTON...

 No.

NO.

NOOOOOOOO!

That's what the inside of my brain sounded like when I realized Rafe and I had spent the past twelve minutes riding that subway train in the wrong direction. Now we were twice as far from the National Mall as when we'd started.

"Please mind the closing doors!" said an announcer's voice.

"Off! Off! Off!" Rafe said, and we bolted off that train before it could take us even farther away.

"What now?" I asked. We were down to our last sixteen minutes. "There's no way I'm going to get this paperwork back to Mrs. Bash on time."

"Unless…" Rafe said. He had this look on his face like he was trying to do complex math in his head, even though he probably wasn't. Everyone knows Rafe hates math.

"Unless what?" I asked.

"Well, maybe…" he said, still thinking.

"Maybe what?"

"Hmm," he said, starting to pace. "I think I'm getting an idea."

"Can you get it a little faster?" I asked. "The clock is ticking."

"Give me your phone," Rafe said. "And hold up that permit. Maybe we *can* get it back there in time, after all."

I didn't bother asking more questions. Every second counted now. So I gave Rafe my phone and held up the permit in my hands.

"Say cheese!" Rafe said, as he pointed the camera my way.

"Cheese!"

"Not you. I was talking to the permit," Rafe said, and snapped a close-up of the paperwork. Then he gave me back my phone. "Now text that—"

"To Mrs. Bash!" I said, finally catching on.

Already, I was texting that picture to the number on her business card.

Then I called her.

"Violet Bash," she answered.

"It's Jimmy!" I said. "Did you get the picture I just sent?"

"I certainly did," she said.

"Great! So then—"

"And I can't read a single word of it," she snapped.

"Oh."

"Not on this little phone screen," she said. "This could be a picture of a candy bar wrapper, for all I know."

"But it's not!" I said.

"But it could be," she said.

I wanted to punch a wall or something, but that seemed like it might hurt. So I just cut the call abruptly.

When I told Rafe what the deal was, he went right back into scheming mode. I could see the same look on his face as before.

"There has to be something we can do," he said. "Otherwise, Mrs. Bash is going to start shutting us down in…"

He looked at me.

I looked at my watch.

"Fourteen minutes!" I said.

"Unless..." Rafe said.

"Unless what?" I asked.

"Well, maybe..." he said.

"RAFE!" I said. "Skip ahead!"

So he told me what he was thinking, and I got right on it. I texted the same picture as before, but to Storm this time. Then I called her instead of Mrs. Bash.

"Jimmy, where *are* you?" Storm asked.

"Not important," I said. "Listen, you know the big jumbotron screens on either side of the stage?"

"Uh, yeah? They're kind of hard to miss," she said.

"I need you to take the picture I just sent you and patch it straight up to those screens," I said. "You'll know what to do after that."

"On it!" Storm said. I heard some clicking on her laptop. Then I heard her voice again. "Excuse me, Mrs. Bash? Can you please look right up at that screen?"

I couldn't see what was happening, but I could imagine it.

"Jimmy? I'm putting Mrs. Bash on the line," Storm told me.

Then I heard Mrs. Bash herself. "All right, young man, because I am feeling generous, I will allow you a one-hour grace period to bring me the hard copy of that permit," she said. "This is your final warning. Do you understand? *One hour.*"

"We'll see you in *less* than that!" I said.

All we had to do now was catch that subway in the other direction, and we'd be back at the National Mall in plenty of time. Nobody would have to shut anything down, and this whole day could still be 100% awesome.

Yes!

YES!

YESSSSS!

CHAPTER 36

UP AND AT IT

Ladies and gentlemen, step right up and get a look at…

Me.

At four inches tall on my hind feet, and somewhere around three-quarters of an ounce of pure mouse muscle, I am Isaiah, possibly the world's smartest rodent. I speak both Mouse and English, as you can probably tell by now.

And no, your eyes aren't fooling you. My fur is indeed bright blue. I'm just one of many hundreds like me, in all different colors. You can blame the laboratory where I was born for that little quirk.

Happily enough, we don't live there anymore. We were taken in by another mischief—which means a family of mice. So now we live in the basement and walls of a home owned by some humans named Brophy.

That's where this tale of adventure begins. On a not-so-normal morning in the Brophy basement, as I woke to the sounds of footsteps overhead.

And doors slamming.

And then a car engine roaring off into the distance.

It was barely the crack of dawn, and the Brophys are not usually the early-riser types. They're more like the get-up-at-noon-and-turn-on-the-television types. So I knew something was strange before I even opened my eyes and saw one of our mischief elders, James the Wise, looking down at me.

"Good news, Isaiah," he said. "I've come from the southwest lookout, and the Brophys just left the house. With *luggage.*"

Luggage! Now *there's* a great word, mostly because of what it meant for us. Anytime the Brophys went away carrying those strange canvas bags and leather boxes, it meant they weren't coming back for *at least* a day. Usually more.

Which meant no humans guarding the kitchen.

Which meant nonstop snacking for the rest of us.

I was already thinking about what I wanted to eat. I'm not picky, but I am a particular fan of cream horns. And Doritos. And cream horns topped with Dorito crumbs. Or Doritos topped with cream horn crumbs. You get the idea.

"Take a small scouting team and make sure the coast is clear," James the Wise told me. "Then send word back when it's safe to start sending up eating parties."

"Yes, sir!" I said. A new adventure plus the promise of unlimited eating? Now *that's* worth getting out of bed for.

"Hey, Gregory! Mikayla!" I shouted to my friends across the sleeping burrow.

Gregory lifted his head from the pickle jar lid mounded with old yarn where he slept, and Mikayla came running from the other room, because she's always up early.

"Is it true?" she asked. "I heard the Brophys left with *luggage*!"

"You heard correctly!" I said, and we high-four'd

all around. (Because we mice have four toes on our front paws, not five.)

Oh my, oh my, oh my. It was going to be a great day.

CHAPTER 37

THE SCOUTING PARTY

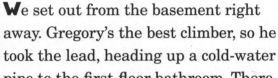 **W**e set out from the basement right away. Gregory's the best climber, so he took the lead, heading up a cold-water pipe to the first-floor bathroom. There are dozens of ways to get around that house, but this route gave us the most cover. Just in case.

One by one, we squeezed through a tiny hole in the bathroom floor, behind the toilet. Then we stopped to listen and sniff.

"I don't smell anyone," Gregory said.

"Me neither," Mikayla said. "I don't hear anything, either."

The house was as quiet as a…well, I won't say mouse, because I know some really noisy mice. But it sure sounded empty.

We proceeded out to the hall and looked both

ways before we crossed. Then we skittered along the baseboard toward the kitchen.

"I'm so excited!" Mikayla said. "I just want to eat butter all day!"

"I hope they left some of those little cocktail wieners in the sink again," Gregory added.

I was thinking about Doritos and cream horns, of course, but not for long. As soon as we got into the kitchen, we stopped short.

Something was wrong. The kitchen floor was... spotless. Not a crumb in sight. It was just clean linoleum as far as the eye could see. And if you knew the Brophys, you'd know how strange that was. Usually, they left a delicious mess everywhere they went. *Especially* in the kitchen.

"I just got a chill all the way down my tail," Gregory said.

"Let's not give up yet," Mikayla said. "Maybe there's still something up top."

It was impossible to see the counters from where we were, so we set out in three different directions to investigate. I shimmied up the leg of a bar stool, jumped over to a dish towel hanging on a hook, and pulled myself up next to the stove, hoping for a little baked-on cheese or at least some burned toast crumbs by the toaster.

But nope.

"Nothing in the trash can!" Gregory reported out.

"And nothing here, either," Mikayla called from the edge of the sink. "No pizza crusts, no dried ketchup on plates. In fact, no plates at all. It looks like they washed the dishes and put them away."

"Why would they do that?" Gregory asked.

"This is getting creepier by the second," I said.

And that's when we heard the slam of another car door outside.

Everyone froze.

"Do you think they're back?" Gregory whispered.

"Hang on," Mikayla said. She hopped to the windowsill above the sink and peeked out.

"It's not the Brophys," she said. "It's a man I've never seen before."

"What's he doing?" Gregory asked from the lip of the trash can.

"Taking things out of his van," she told us. "The back of his uniform says...*Sunshine...something.*"

"'Sunshine *something*'?" Gregory asked.

"I don't recognize the second word," Mikayla said. Not everyone in our mischief is as good with English as I am.

"Sunshine Bakery?" I suggested hopefully.

"Sunshine Pizza?" Gregory asked.

"I don't think so," Mikayla answered. "It starts with an *E*."

"What are the rest of the letters?" I asked.

"Let's see," she said, and squinted out the window. "It says *Sunshine...E-X-T-E-R-M-I-N-A-T-O-R-S.*"

CHAPTER 38

SOS!

Go warn the others," I said. "Start getting everyone out of the burrow! Every last mouse!"

"Why? What was that word?" Mikayla asked.

I didn't have the heart to tell her what an exterminator was. It could cause a panic down below, and that was the last thing we needed right now.

"Just go tell everyone to evacuate the burrow—*now*."

"All two thousand eight hundred and thirty of them?" Gregory asked. "But that's going to take—"

"NOW!" I bellowed. "And I'm going to call for reinforcements."

We still had a secret weapon we might be able

to use. Her name was Hailey, and she lived across the street from the Brophys. If I had to choose a best friend in the world who *didn't* have whiskers and a tail, it would be no contest. Hailey had saved our little hides more than once before.

So while Mikayla and Gregory ran back up the hall, I ran the other way, to the room the Brophys called the den.

The door was closed when I got there, but mice are pretty bendy that way. I squeezed myself against the floor, as flat as I could, and wriggled right inside.

From there, it was a quick sprint through some shag carpet that came to my ears. Then I scrambled up the front of the sofa, across a seat cushion, and straight up again, until I was on top of the world.

Well, on top of the couch, anyway. It was a long way down from there.

Now came the hard part—a giant leap over to the desktop, where the computer lived. I'd done this before, but it always made me nervous.

Still, when I heard the front door creak open, followed by the heavy, clomping footsteps of the exterminator himself, I found all the courage I needed.

I crouched down hard, took a deep breath—and leaped.

For a brief moment, it was like flying.

Then I hit the smooth desktop like a patch of ice and skidded out. If I hadn't collided with the computer keyboard, I would have slid right off the back of the desk and into the octopus tangle of cords that lived there. It had happened once before and took me hours to get free.

Right now, I didn't have hours. I didn't even have minutes. For all I knew, the exterminator was going to throw open that den door any second. I felt like I was in one of those loud, suspenseful movies the Brophys always watched.

Mouse-sion: Impossible!

It took a few taps on the space bar to wake the computer. Then I shoved the mouse (the other kind) until it was pointing at the MESSAGES icon on the screen. A hard double stomp got the software to click open, and I was in.

Now it was back to the keyboard, skipping across some keys and stomping on others, as I put in my user name—ISAIAH—and password—DORITOS—to access the account Hailey had set up for me.

As for my actual message, I kept it short and simple. Although I did turn the exclamation point key into a kind of trampoline, jumping up and down many times for emphasis.

SOS!!!!!!!!!!!!!!

I think that got the idea across. And thank goodness, Hailey answered right away.

Be right there!

Now I just had to get back down to the burrow, where I could help with the evacuation.

Assuming I didn't meet an untimely end before I got there.

CHAPTER 39

REINFORCEMENTS

**B**ack in the tiny space under the den door, I stopped and looked around.

Sure enough, there he was! The Sunshine Exterminator man, who looked like anything but sunshine to me, was using a flashlight to spy under the kitchen sink. And there was only one thing he might be looking for. *Victims.*

He kept looking up, making marks on his clipboard, and then poking that flashlight into another corner.

I knew we had to stop him. I just didn't know how yet.

As I scanned the area some more, I also saw where he'd dropped a mask, some goggles, and a gray metal tank with a long spray arm. Something

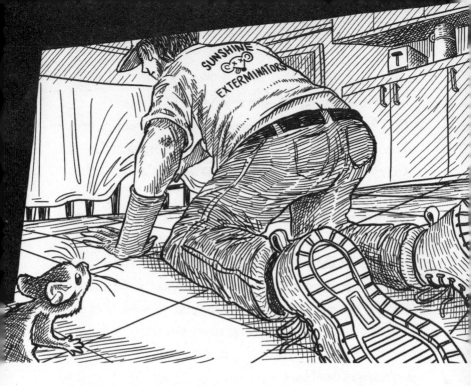

told me that tank wasn't filled with Cheez Whiz, either.

I stayed there, waiting on a chance to make a break for the bathroom. When you're bright blue, you need to be extra careful about blending in. Especially for human eyes.

Finally, I saw my chance. The exterminator man had just opened the oven door and stuck his head deep inside for a look. That's when I went for it. I sprinted straight up the hall, into the bathroom—and then smack dab into Mikayla.

"What are you doing up here?" I shouted.

"I had to come back and make sure you were okay," Mikayla said. "Gregory's getting word to the others, and they're all evacuating right now. But we need more time!"

I knew there was no chance of being overheard. Mice have ultrasonic voices. The only way for them to be picked up by human ears is for a whole mischief to speak at once. So we were safe, for now.

"Go back and keep evacuating," I said. "I'll see if I can't create some kind of diversion."

"Isaiah, no!" Mikayla put her paws on me. "It's too dangerous!"

I was about to argue, but then we were interrupted by a knock at the Brophys' screen door.

"Hello?" came a voice. The most welcome voice I could imagine. "Anybody home?"

Hailey!

CHAPTER 40

IT TAKES A MISCHIEF

We stood frozen in the bathroom doorway, watching as the exterminator man went to see who was there. The name patch on his chest said GUS.

As in "disGUSting!"

And "boGUS!"

And "go away and leave us alone, GUS!"

"Can I help you?" Gus asked. "You shouldn't be hanging around here today, little girl."

"Oh, sorry," Hailey said. "It's just...well..." She was looking around, past the man and down the hall, while his back was to me. So I stepped out to where she could see me for a moment, just long enough to wave.

Hailey's eyes got wide. The man turned to see what she was looking at, but I'm quick that way. I'd already made myself scarce once again.

Meanwhile, my heart was going like a hummingbird's.

"Sorry," Hailey said to him. "It's just, I saw your truck, and I find this all so *interesting*. You know, my dad used to be an exterminator."

"That right?" Gus asked, but he sounded unimpressed.

"Yeah," Hailey said. "I mean…" She paused again, and I saw her face change, like she'd just gotten an idea. "That was until the side effects of all that spray poison started kicking in."

Now Gus was paying attention. "Huh?" he asked.

"I'm sure you've heard the stories," Hailey went on, with another look my way. "Seeing *colors,* hearing *voices*. They say that's why exterminating is such a short career. But you already knew that, right?"

And I realized, she wasn't just stalling. She was sending me a secret message in the only way she knew how.

I turned to Mikayla again. "Change of plans," I squeaked. "Go down and get as many of my family up here as possible. At least ten of every color!"

A second later, she'd disappeared under the bathroom floor, and I went back to listening.

"Gimme a break!" Gus said. "I've been doing this for years, and I'm fine."

"I'm not kidding!" Hailey said. "My dad had to get another job."

I knew Hailey liked to do plays at school, and she's a good actress. No—a great actress. But still, Gus didn't seem too impressed.

"Listen, kid. You need to get away from this work site," he said. He pulled something off his clipboard and held it up to show her. "You see this big green ALL CLEAR sticker? When I put that up in the front window, it means the house has been treated and it's okay to come back inside."

I shuddered at the sight of it, because I knew what *ALL CLEAR* meant. It meant "no more mice."

Meanwhile, my colorful relatives were starting to pour into the bathroom. They were coming from behind the toilet, under the sink, and beneath the heat register. Already, we had at least three dozen mice in eight different colors, waiting to see what happened next.

"In the meantime," Gus told Hailey, as he picked up his gray tank of poison, "you need to vamoose."

"But—" Hailey said.

"Go on. Scram. I've got work to do."

And this is where the responsibility fell back to me, I realized. I'm pretty good with words, as you may have noticed, and I already had a plan.

"Now, repeat after me!" I shouted to the family. "One-two-three-four! Go away! Walk out the door!"

And everyone did, in a big mouse chorus. Big enough even for human ears.

"ONE-TWO-THREE-FOUR! GO AWAY! WALK OUT THE DOOR!"

I held up a foot to quiet everyone again, and we listened.

"What was that?" I heard the man say.

"What was what? I didn't hear anything," Hailey said, even though I knew she had.

And then I went again.

"Two-four-six-eight! It's wrong to exterminate!" I chanted, before the others joined in.

"TWO-FOUR-SIX-EIGHT! IT'S WRONG TO EXTERMINATE!"

"That!" the man yelled. "It's like…tiny high-pitched voices!"

"ONE-TWO-THREE-FOUR! GO AWAY! WALK OUT THE DOOR!"

"Oh, mister, I'm so sorry," Hailey said.

"TWO-FOUR-SIX-EIGHT! IT'S WRONG TO EXTERMINATE!"

"This is exactly what happened to my dad after working with all those chemicals and poisons," she kept going.

"They're perfectly safe if you know how to handle them," Gus said. But he didn't sound so convinced anymore.

"Next thing you know, you'll start seeing strange *colors,* too," Hailey told him.

And that was our cue for the next part. There was no time to waste. So I turned and squeaked out a new command at the top of my lungs.

"Now *CHARGE!*" I roared.

And that's exactly what we did.

CHAPTER 41

CHARGE!

 **I** led the charge, with a furry rainbow pouring out of the bathroom behind me. We all ran straight at Gus as we headed for the open front door.

"What the…?" Gus screamed. "Tell me you're seeing this!"

"All those gray mice?" Hailey asked. She'd jumped up on a chair, just to add to her performance. "Yes, I see them! Ewwwww! How disgusting!" She was really pouring it on but gave me a sly wink as I passed by.

"No!" Gus said. "I mean…they're blue! And yellow…and green…and…"

He raised a foot to stomp down on whoever was passing by at the time—including me. I looked up and saw the tread of his boot coming my way, just before Hailey screamed again. She pretended to fall off her chair and fell right into Gus, knocking both of them to the floor. His clipboard hit the ground with a piercing smack as he scrambled back onto his feet and stumbled away, into the den. It was just the diversion we needed, while the family continued on toward the freedom of the outdoors.

But then I realized there was one more thing I could do. Something worth doubling back for. So I turned around and ran upstream, against everyone else going the other way.

I went straight for Gus's clipboard on the floor. It was that ALL CLEAR sticker I wanted, and I bit down hard, trying to tug it free from the clip. But it wouldn't budge. That clip was bigger than I was.

"A little help?" I squeaked.

The next thing I knew, Mikayla and Gregory were right there. They took up positions on either side of the clip, while I stayed with my jaws locked around that awful decal.

"One, two, three—heave!" Mikayla said. They pushed, and pressed, and lifted the clip, just far enough off the board that I could slide the sticker free. A few moments later, we were disappearing with it out the front door and around the side of the house.

As soon as we were out of sight, we stopped and turned back to watch.

"I'm out of here!" Gus was shouting, as Hailey trailed after him, trying not to laugh.

"Maybe a career in real estate?" she asked. "That's what my dad does now."

He threw his poison tank in the back of the van, jumped in the front seat, and took off like he was never coming back.

Which of course was the whole idea.

CHAPTER 42

HOME SWEET HOME

Everyone was cheering now. Gregory and Mikayla hoisted me on their shoulders. They carried me back around to the front, where Hailey was just coming to find us. She took the ALL CLEAR sticker from me and put it right there in the front window. Then she locked the Brophys' door and left the house as though she'd never been there in the first place.

"Way to go, Isaiah!" she said. If she'd had her laptop with her, I could have spelled out my thanks in oh-so-many words. Instead, I just blew a kiss and a big smile her way, but I think she got my drift.

So now that we'd figured out how to save our

entire mischief from a disaster of epic proportions, there was still the *second* most important question of the day.

"What's for breakfast?" Gregory asked. "I'm starving, and that kitchen is as empty as a hatched egg."

"We'll be just fine," said James the Wise, who was there now to congratulate us. "Everything the Brophys took out of the kitchen is in the trash bins behind the garage. There's more than enough to feast on for the time being."

Which sounded just great to me. Everything always tastes better outdoors anyway.

As for the Brophys? When they came back, I don't think they even noticed that the ALL CLEAR sticker in their window had a few tiny teeth marks around the edges. It didn't take long for them to return to their deliciously sloppy ways around the house, either. We're being extra careful these days, but life has gone fairly well back to normal.

It's certainly possible that we'll have to go looking for a new home someday. But if it comes to that, I'm confident that my mighty mischief will be up to the task.

And you know me. I'm *always* ready for a new adventure.

CHAPTER 43

THE BIRTHDAY PARTY CONUNDRUM

 I have a question for everybody listening. Do you ever wonder how we got here? Like, once upon a time, there was nothing but a bunch of microorganisms swimming on the bottom of the ocean. Then fast-forward four billion years, and here I am on the National Mall in Washington, DC, with planes flying in the sky and a tiny computer in everyone's pocket.

Crazy, right?

I can't account for everything that's happened in the past four billion years, but I can explain how I came to be here on this stage, telling my story. It all started a week before my last birthday, when my friend Ben asked, "So, Max? What does a world-class genius like you want for her special day?"

"World peace," I answered. "An end to the global water crisis. Improved infrastructure through all of Sub-Saharan Africa."

"Actually, I was just wondering what kind of party you might want to have," Ben said.

"Oh," I said. "Right."

I don't actually know Ben's real name. I just call him Ben, which is short for "benefactor." He's the fourteen-year-old billionaire who funds the projects I help run at the Change Makers Institute. He also provided me with my apartment in New York City, where I live.

Some of you may be familiar with our work, all of it done by kids like me and all of it about tackling the world's big problems. I've led teams taking on green power solutions in the Congo, childhood hunger in Thailand, and clinic building on four continents, to name a few.

So as you can see, no problem is too big for us. Not if we work together. But sometimes, it's the little things that really stump me.

"I'm not sure," I told Ben. "I've never had one. What are those supposed to be like?"

"It can be whatever you want," Ben said.

And I thought, *Hmmm.* I let my mind run like a Google image search and pulled up a bunch of places where I imagined birthday parties might happen.

At the park?

In a video game arcade?

Indoor skydiving arena?

Medieval dinner?

"What about that escape room place over on 23rd Street?" I asked Ben. "That might be fun. And it's kind of what we do at Change Makers anyway. You know, figuring out solutions to things."

"I'd think something like that wouldn't be much of a challenge for someone with your IQ," Ben said.

I don't know what my IQ is, since I've never had it tested. But I'd never been to an escape room, either.

"Let's check it out," I said. "If we like it, we have the party there next week."

"Sounds good," Ben said, as we headed out the door. "And if it's not fun, then I know you'll come up with another idea."

Well, at least I'll always try.

CHAPTER 44

TEST RUN

This looks cool," I said, as we lined up with our group at NYC-Escapes on 23rd Street an hour later. Ben had let me choose which room, and I'd picked the one called "The Haunted Library."

"The others sound good too," I said, just as a lady in a bright yellow NYC-Escapes shirt called over our group. Ben and I were with a family of four—a mom, a dad, a boy about my age, and a younger sister. This was going to be fun!

"Okay, everyone!" the lady said. "Once you're inside, remember you need to work quickly to find clues, solve the series of puzzles, and figure out how to get out of the Haunted Library in *sixty minutes or less,*" she said. "Got that?"

"Yes!" we said.

"Is everyone excited?" she asked.

"YES!" we answered. I really was. There was something so...*normal* about this. And when your life is as abnormal as mine, normal can be exciting.

"Let's do this!" the little girl said. She even gave me a high five. Nice!

Then we followed the lady through a big vault door into what looked like an old-fashioned study.

Right away, I started cataloging everything I saw. I was looking for clues and taking stock from the second I walked in.

I saw maps on the wall. A desk full of papers. Two easy chairs, with a chess game set up on a table. I noticed the checkerboard floor matched the chessboard.

I also saw a wall safe with a combination lock...a fake stuffed lion head mounted on the wall...two half-burned candles—

"Okay, everyone!" the lady said. "Good luck, and your time starts...now!"

She pressed a button on the wall, and a digital clock next to it started ticking down from sixty minutes.

Then she pulled the vault door closed from the

outside—*KA-CHUNG!*—and locked us in.

"This is exciting!" the mom said.

"Where do you think we should start?" the son asked.

I was still making a list of clues in my head, but I did have a couple of things figured out already.

"Actually, I have an idea," I said. "Do you all mind if I try something?"

"Go for it!" the dad said.

So I did.

THREE-AND-A-HALF MINUTES LATER...

"And *that* gives us the combination to the final lock on this door!" I said, as I completed the last puzzle.

We all heard a loud click. Then the main exit door slowly swung open.

"Yes! We escaped!" I said.

But when I tried to get another high five from the little girl, she just looked at me.

"I thought we had an hour," the mother said.

"An hour or *less*," I said. "I'll bet we just set some kind of record!"

"Well, *you* did," the boy told me.

"You didn't even let us help," the girl said. "Thanks a lot, lady."

"I'm not a 'lady,'" I told her. "I'm a kid too."

"Whatever," she said, just as the disappointed family walked out ahead of us.

"What did I do?" I asked Ben. "I mean, was I supposed to *not* notice that if we used the first letter of all the circled countries on that map, they would spell out 'BLACK KING'? In which case, why *wouldn't* I look at the black king on that chessboard, and why wouldn't I use the numbers on the bottom of the king to open the wall safe—"

Ben held up a hand. "Yes, I know. You got through it all really fast. But the idea was to let *everyone* have a good time too."

"Oh, yeah," I said. "Right." I was getting embarrassed now. I guess I really had gotten carried away. But that's what happens to me when it comes to problem solving. Once my brain revs up, I just can't slow it down.

In fact, some part of my mind was already moving on to the next thing. Because that's what I do. I solve problems.

But sometimes, I don't realize I'm the one causing them.

CHAPTER 45

LET'S TRY THAT AGAIN

 **D**on't worry about it," Ben told me as we walked home. "I spoke to the escape room people and arranged for that family to receive a year's worth of gift certificates."

"Great—thank you," I said. I still felt bad about how it had gone.

"I also assured them you wouldn't be coming back," he added with a laugh.

Ben had been right all along. Those escape rooms weren't exactly a challenge for me. But like any good scientist, now I was examining where I'd gone wrong, so I could try a new approach.

Then another circuit fired somewhere in my brain. And another. And another. Really, there were tens of millions of brain cells at work. Not that it makes me special. You have millions of brain cells firing all the time too.

Still, I'd already taken the last idea, zoomed in on it, broken it down to its components, zoomed out, looked at what I had, and rearranged the pieces into something new.

That's what my idol, Albert Einstein (no relation—I think), had always done. It's called "combinatory play." He took the pieces of things he already knew about and he played with them, rearranging and combining the different ingredients until he came up with an idea worth having.

Which is exactly what I did as we walked home.

"I can tell you're thinking about something," Ben said. "Did you come up with a new idea for your party?"

"Kind of," I said. "More like a new version of the old idea."

"You mean you *still* want to go to an escape room?" he asked, sounding surprised.

"Not exactly," I said. "Now I want to *create* an escape room."

"Ah," he said. "That makes more sense."

"And not just a regular escape room," I went on, and told him everything I was thinking.

Before I was even done explaining, Ben was all over it. Already, he had his phone out. "I'll pull together the team," he said. "You have one week until your actual birthday. You think you can be ready?"

"Oh, I know I can," I said.

In other words, the great birthday party experiment wasn't over. It was just getting started.

CHAPTER 46

PARTY...iSH

"**T**hanks for coming to my party, guys!" I told the team once we were all assembled a week later. There were six of us, like the last time in the escape room, but I knew everyone on this team. This was our New York–based team for the Change Makers Institute. Everyone in the room was fourteen or younger, and most of us had already been through college.

"If this is a party, why are we meeting in an empty warehouse?" Ajit asked, looking around at the concrete floor, high ceiling, and sliding metal door at one end.

"Technically, the room's not empty," I said. We had six chairs, a table, a whiteboard with markers, and a laptop on the table in front of me. "And I'm calling it a party, but it's more like a test run for the new escape rooms I want to create."

Everyone looked around at one another.

"Um...same question," Darcy said. "What's with the nearly empty warehouse?"

"If this is an escape room, where are the clues?" Oliver asked.

"Where are the puzzles?" Kana asked.

"And why does this feel like a work meeting?" Ajit added.

"Here's the idea," I said. "In an escape room, you have to solve a challenge in order to get out, right?"

"Yeah?" Ajit said.

"And that's basically what we all do with the Change Makers Institute," I said. "Right? We work as a team to solve problems."

"Ohhhhh," Kana said. I could see some of them were starting to get it.

"So in other words," I said, "first we pick a challenge, and then we solve it. And *that's* how we escape. It's a Change Makers Escape Room."

"Or something," Ben said. "We're still working on the name. But everything else is ready to go for our first test."

And with that, Ben took a remote out of his pocket and pushed a few buttons. The main door swung closed with a clang. The automated locks we'd had installed clicked shut. And the countdown clock on my laptop automatically started ticking down from sixty minutes.

"You have one hour," Ben said.

"How do we know when we've solved the problem?" Darcy asked.

"When everyone agrees," I said. "It's as simple— or as hard—as that."

Ben added one more point from there. "Our mission has always been about getting kids involved in this kind of work. So if this goes well today, we'll roll this program into schools across the country, getting students to come up with solutions to the world's biggest problems."

"Not only that," I said, "but if anyone comes up with something really good, Ben will fund that project, and we'll get on it ASAP."

"Cool!" Oliver said.

"Why didn't you say so?" Kana asked.

"Let's go, let's go!" Darcy said. "The clock's already ticking!"

"Does this mean there's not going to be any cake?" Oliver asked.

Ben and I looked at each other. Oops. I guess we'd forgotten about that part.

And hey, it may not have been like *your* birthday parties. But this was exactly what I wanted to be doing with mine.

So we jumped right in.

CHAPTER 47

READING THE ROOM

First things first," I said. "What problem do you guys think we should tackle?"

"It's your party, Max," Ajit said. "You can choose."

I thought about it for a second. I really did want this to be a group effort. And since this was at least *supposed* to be a birthday thing, I wanted to do something fun.

"Well," I said, "one of my favorite Albert Einstein quotes says that imagination is more important than knowledge."

I stopped there, just to see what everyone else would say.

"So..." Darcy jumped in. "Maybe we could

do something to help people have better imaginations?"

"Maybe something more specific than that," Kana said.

"What about something with books and reading?" Ajit asked. "That's how you increase imagination."

"Yes!" I said. I liked where this was going already.

"In fact," Kana said, "that fits right in with the Change Makers' mission. Increased literacy and access to reading material have been shown to positively impact poverty, community health, crime rates, and all kinds of other things."

"That reminds me of another Einstein quote," I told everyone. "He once said, 'If you want your children to be intelligent, read them fairy tales. If you want them to be very intelligent, read them more fairy tales.'"

"So that's our challenge!" Kana said. "Literacy! And books! And reading!"

"I love it," Darcy said. "The more kids read—"

"The better off the whole world will be," Ajit said.

So now everyone was on board. Ben, too, who was observing from the corner and nodding.

"Keep going, guys. You still have forty-nine minutes to figure out how you're going to tackle this."

And the brainstorming went on from there.

"We could build a library somewhere," Kana suggested.

"Or have some kind of books-by-mail program," Darcy added.

"Or a reading and writing conference for kids in cities across the country," Ajit jumped in.

"Yes, yes, and yes!" I said.

It was like popcorn now, with ideas popping and flying all over the room while I put them down in the laptop and Ajit scribbled everything on the board.

I felt like we were really homing in on something big. But there was still one missing ingredient.

"How do we make kids *want* to read?" I asked, with only a few minutes left in our hour. "How do we get them interested in the first place?"

"With really good books," Darcy said.

"Ones they'll want to read."

"I like *all* of this. But there should be something big and fun, too," I said. "Some kind of event. Some kind of party."

"Some kind of *worldwide* reading party!" Kana said.

It was all just a big yes, yes, YES. And in fact, I was starting to think maybe I was just one phone call away from our solution.

CHAPTER 48

FULL CIRCLE

 **S**o, can you guess who I called next?

And can you guess what happened after that (I mean besides our getting out of that escape room on time)?

I'll wait. Go ahead and guess.

If you're still stumped, just look around you. Because it took me all of one minute on the phone with Jimmy before he was as excited about this idea as we were.

And Ben was completely on board too. He put up the funding for this whole celebration, while Jimmy took care of the rest. In fact, this event is the first official project that's come out of the Change Makers Escape Room Subdivision.

Or maybe we'll call it Kids Think, Inc.

Or something. We're *still* working on the name.

But who knows, maybe we'll be coming to a school near you sometime soon. And maybe you and your friends will come up with some great ideas of your own. In fact, I'm counting on it.

Because from where I'm standing, the future looks brighter than ever!

And sweeter, too. Because by the way, there's free cake for everyone now, at the concession stands all over the Mall. Just tell them Max sent you!

And happy birthday to me!

CHAPTER 49

PEDAL TO THE METAL

 **R**afe and I had our eyes glued to my phone during all of Isaiah's and then Max Einstein's stories. I don't even know which of those two geniuses is smarter.

When I finally did look up, I realized we'd been waiting for that train to take us back in the right direction for a long time. Too long. The subway platform was filling up with people. A lot of them were looking up the tunnel for a train that didn't seem to be coming.

"I don't have a good feeling about this," Rafe said.

And then sure enough, an announcement blared over the station loudspeaker.

"Attention, passengers! Due to mechanical

failure, trains on this line will be out of service for thirty to sixty minutes."

"WHAT?" I said.

"He said thirty to sixty minutes," Rafe told me.

"No, I heard that part," I said. "It's just that we can't risk waiting anymore. Mrs. Bash only gave us an hour to get back. So what do we do now?"

Rafe thumbed toward the escalator. "We go upstairs to the street for starters," he said. "Unless you want to—"

"Don't even say it," I told him. "We're not walking into that subway tunnel."

"Could have been kind of cool," Rafe said, as we started to follow the other people out of the station. "But whatever. We'll come up with something else."

When we got to the street, I stopped and looked around. We had to get back to the National Mall one way or another. But how? I wished Kenny Wright were with us. He knew the city better than anyone. But Kenny was getting ready to tell his story next on the main stage.

Which meant Rafe and I were on our own.

"The traffic is even more insane than before," I said, looking up and down the street. "It's too far to walk. And the subway's a no-go. What does that leave?"

"RENT ME!" Rafe shouted all of a sudden.

"Huh?" I asked. "Why would I rent you?"

But Rafe wasn't listening. He was pointing at something. And then he was running after something. I had to sprint to catch up.

"Excuse me!" Rafe was yelling as he went. "EXCUSE ME! WHERE DID YOU GET THAT?"

I thought he'd officially lost his mind for a second there. But then I saw what he was chasing.

Just ahead, there was a girl riding up the street on an orange bike. And on the side of that bike was a sign that said CAPITOL WHEELS. RENT ME!

He caught up to her now and said something to her without either of them stopping. She pointed back the way we'd just come, and then Rafe hurried back in my direction.

"Twoblocksthisway!" he said as he zoomed past. All I could do was turn one-eighty and keep following, until we came to a big rack of those same orange bikes.

It was only a dollar to rent each bike, but you needed a credit card. Which I actually had.

"My parents gave it to me for the trip to Washington," I said. "But they told me it was for emergencies only."

"Um, hello?" Rafe said. "If this isn't an emergency, I don't know what is."

"Good point," I said, and stuck my credit card in the machine. Thirty seconds later, we had two bikes and helmets, and we took off riding...for about ten feet. That's when I remembered we still didn't know which way to go.

Duh!

"Excuse me!" I said to a lady on a park bench. "Which way is the National Mall?"

The lady gave me a funny look. I wondered if maybe I had food on my face or something.

"Aren't you Jimmy?" she asked.

"That's him!" Rafe said. "He's the story kid!"

"I know!" she said, and held up her phone, where I could see she was watching the show. "What are you doing all the way over here?"

"Trying to get back!" I said. "ASAP, in fact!"

"Head that way on Nebraska Avenue," the lady told me, and pointed up the street. "When you get to Massachusetts Avenue, take a left. Then right on 23rd, and keep going until you see the National Mall. Then left on Constitution Avenue, and you're almost there."

"Have you got all that?" I asked Rafe.

"Uh…I think so," he said.

It was a start, anyway. So I thanked the lady and we took off again.

"*Go, Jimmy, go!*" the lady yelled. "And good luck!"

I'm not going to lie. That felt pretty awesome. Now we just had to get back to where we were trying to go…

Once.

And.

For.

All!

CHAPTER 50

EVASIVE MANEUVERS

 **S**o there I was, running down the hall of Union Middle School like my life depended on it. Which it basically did, with Tiny Simpkins closing in on me fast.

It's not even like I'd done anything to him. More like Tiny "Don't Let the Name Fool You" Simpkins ate sixth graders for breakfast, lunch, and dinner. And I was his midmorning snack.

"Yeah, you better run!" Tiny shouted. I knew that tone in his voice, too. It said, "Kenny Wright wants to spend some quality time in his locker."

So I kept moving. I ran up one hall and down another and cut a hard right into a side corridor, through the cafeteria, and up the back stairs. And the whole time, I was thinking one thing—

What would Stainlezz Steel do?

Stainlezz Steel is the superhero I only *wish* I could be. I'm weak, and Steel is strong. I'm stuck on the ground, and Steel can fly. I'm scared silly of Tiny Simpkins, and Steel? He's not scared of anything.

In fact, I knew exactly what Steel would do. He'd fly a lap around that school so fast, he'd be coming up on Tiny's back before Tiny even knew it was happening. Flash forward another microsecond, and there's Tiny with his head stuck in the ceiling tiles, wondering how the lights went out so quick.

But like I said, Steel's not for real. He just lives inside my head. When it came to *actually* dealing with Tiny Simpkins, I was on my own. So I kept running and headed for the third floor without even looking back.

Believe me, I know about evasive maneuvers. I'm used to being chased by bullies. I'm also pretty good at chess, and that game's all about making sure you don't get cornered by the other guy.

Even so, I knew I couldn't compete with Tiny's long legs. I was still waiting on that mythical growth spurt my grandma said was coming. And in the meantime, the only thing growing was the chance of my spending the rest of that morning inside my locker.

Because if life is just a game of chess, then I'm a pawn living in a world of kings and queens.

CHAPTER 51

NON-SMOOTH TALKER

The good news? I didn't have to wait long before someone let me out of my locker.

The bad news? Shuly Williams was the one to do it.

Talk about embarrassing!

"Hey, Kenny," she said. "I saw what that fool did. Don't worry about him."

"Uh…thanks…um…uh…Shuly," I said.

Shuly was *way* out of my league, but her mom and my grandma (who I call G-ma) went way back. They were always doing things together down at St. Anthony's church. So I'd known her most of my life. Which is also about as long as I'd been in love with her.

"Hey, is your grandma making you work the

church book sale this weekend?" Shuly asked.

G-ma was, but I tried to play it cool. I didn't want to look like a grandma's boy, on top of everything else.

"I don't know," I said. "I might blow it off."

"Oh," she said. "Because I'll be there too—"

"Did I say blow it off?" I asked. "I meant...you know. Blow it *on*. Like, the opposite. Like, uh, yeah, for sure. I'll be there."

That's me, all right. Just as smooth as a chunky peanut butter and gravel sandwich. But Shuly only smiled, because she's nice that way. Even to geeks like me.

"So I guess I'll see you there," she said.

And I thought to myself, *What would Stainlezz Steel say right now?*

But I'm no Stainlezz Steel. So here's what came out instead:

"Uh…yeah. Uh…see you there. For sure. Yeah. Okay. Well…yeah."

Seriously, why does it have to be that way? It's like anytime I'm under a little pressure, my brain just freezes up and I'm gripped with a big case of the doubts.

Which is also where I came up with the idea for a new supervillain in my Stainlezz Steel universe. I call him the Gripper. He's not any stronger than you or me, but he knows exactly how to get into someone's head and mess them up from the inside out. Even someone like Steel.

Here, let me show you what I mean.

CHAPTER 52

MEET THE GRIPPER

It's been a quiet night for Stainlezz Steel so far, patrolling the skies over Washington and keeping the city safe. But just after two in the morning, an alert flashes across the surveillance screen built into his helmet.

SUSPICIOUS ACTIVITY DETECTED. VANDALISM IN PROGRESS. WASHINGTON MONUMENT.

Local Time: 02:05 hours
38.9072°N, 77.0369W
Weather: 17°C
Wind S at 6 km/h
Humidity: 68%
Population: 702,445

Steel banks hard and flies straight to the crime scene, landing there just a few seconds later.

Sure enough, someone's already there and up to no good. This guy has a whole utility belt stocked with cans of spray paint. And is he actually *tagging the Washington Monument?*

Yes, he is.

So far, the dude hasn't even turned around. He's listening to something on the craziest pair of headphones Steel's ever seen.

"I hope you've got some extra time," Steel says. "'Cause you're going to be cleaning that up for the rest of the night."

The guy turns around slowly, like maybe he just heard something. When he sees Steel, he pulls the 'phones off his head.

"Hang on," he says. "I'll be done in just a sec."

He's got some ice in his veins, Steel thinks. *That's for sure.*

"Who are you?" Steel asks.

"Can't you read?" The guy points at his own graffiti. "I'm the Gripper."

"Yeah, well, you're also under arrest," Steel says. "Let's go. *Now.*"

Instead, the Gripper winds up and whips his own headphones straight at Steel. A flash of light and sound fill the air. Steel dodges, but not fast enough. The next thing he knows, something cold and metallic is clamping down onto his skull. Then over his ears, too.

"What the...?" Steel yells. He reaches up to yank the thing off, but he doesn't even get that far. A voice sounds in his ears and stops him.

Give it up, Steel.

"Huh?" he says.

You can't fight this.

Don't even try, you loser.

The even weirder thing is, it's his own voice he's hearing. Like he's talking to himself from the inside out.

Game over, Steel.

You had a good run, but it's time to make way for new blood.

"What...is...this thing?" he asks, gritting his teeth.

"It's my latest brain worm," the Gripper says. "Pretty good, right? It hacks into your mind, and then I don't have to fight you at all, because you fight yourself instead."

Steel tries to reach for the little guy, but he can't. Something's stopping him. He can't even raise an arm, much less throw a punch.

"See what I mean?" the Gripper asks, and leans in close with an evil smile. "I'm kind of a genius, if I do say so myself."

All Steel can do is watch and listen, as the voice—his own voice—worms its way deeper into his mind, crippling him with his own thoughts.

You're finished.

You're weak.

Don't even try.

"You won't…get away…with this," Steel grunts out.

"Except I already have," the Gripper tells him, with a laugh. "Now, if you'll excuse me, the rest of these monuments aren't going to tag themselves."

And all Steel can do is watch as the Gripper moves on, laughing his way toward the next target.

TO BE CONTINUED…

CHAPTER 53

COME SALE AWAY

**S**o that Saturday morning, I was there in the basement of St. Anthony's church, where G-ma and all the ladies were setting up for the big book sale. Mostly, I was wondering when Shuly and her mom were going to show up, but I was also keeping busy.

Or more like G-ma was keeping me busy.

"Kenneth! More books, please!"

My job was to take this mountain of boxes, all filled with donated books, and carry them over to where the ladies were sorting. Like, cookbooks over here, mysteries over there, and the books G-ma wanted to buy for herself (which were a lot) off to the side.

Books are mad heavy, too. And like I said, I'm not exactly the Hulk. So there I was, lugging another big carton, like some kind of baby giraffe on wobbly legs, when guess who walked in?

And if you guessed anyone besides Shuly Williams, guess again.

"Hey, Kenny!" she said.

Which is when my arms decided to stop working. I grunted, and stumbled, and dropped the whole box of books right there on the floor.

And yeah, it got worse. Because just then, my little five-foot-nothing grandma picked up a couple of empty boxes from her side of the room and started carrying them back the other way like they were nothing. Because they *were* nothing. But you couldn't tell that just by looking at the boxes. Which was why Shuly was standing there now, trying not to laugh.

And I thought—

Well, whatever. Who wants to hang out all day with an incredibly smart, pretty, cool girl like Shuly Williams, anyway?

But then I remembered—

Oh, yeah. I do.

CHAPTER 54

A LITTLE HELP?

In a superhero movie, this would be the part of the story where the hero goes to find his mentor and get some ancient wisdom. Kind of like the way Luke Skywalker has Yoda, or the X-Men have Professor X.

I didn't have a Yoda or a Professor X, but I did have Father Daniel. And he was right there at St. Anthony's.

Father Daniel was kind of corny, but if you knew him, you'd know he's got this secret cool side. And he's really smart, too.

So while Shuly, G-ma, and the other ladies were bonding over the books of Jason Reynolds, Crystal Allen, Gene Luen Yang, and all kinds of other awesome writers, I went upstairs to Father Daniel's office.

"Kenneth, come in! What can I do for you?" he asked.

"Well, um…" I hadn't really decided how to tackle this one, so I just spit it out. "To be honest, I was wondering if you had any advice about talking to girls."

Father Daniel nodded with a hand on his chin. "Hypothetically speaking," he said, "might we be talking about Shuly Williams here?"

"We might," I said. "You know. Hypothetically."

"Okay then, let me ask you this: what's Shuly's favorite food?" he asked.

"I don't know," I said.

"Favorite book?"

"Uh…"

"What's her middle name?" he asked.

"I'm supposed to know that, too?" I asked.

"Well, there's your problem right there," he said. "You need to express an interest, son. You may not think so, but girls your age find boys to be very confusing. Sometimes it's best if you make things clear. Respectfully, of course."

It already seemed like a lot to remember. I was kind of wishing I'd brought a paper and pencil.

"So, what do I do first?" I asked.

"Ask questions," he said. "Give her the respect of your curiosity."

And even though Father Daniel had some starter ideas, I still couldn't come up with anything good on my own. I just stood there thinking up one dumb question after another.

"Here's one more thing to think about," Father Daniel said, and put a hand on my shoulder. "More than anything, just be yourself."

I told you he was corny.

"Now you're looking at me like I'm corny," Father Daniel said. "But trust me on this one."

"What if she doesn't like my self?" I asked. "What if she wants some other self?"

Father Daniel spread his hands like that was all he had to give. "Then I guess you don't get the girl. Nobody said it was easy. But in the meantime, who else are you going to be?"

And of course, I thought of Stainlezz Steel.

But I kept my mouth shut about that.

CHAPTER 55

KENNY VS. SHULY

 **S**o about five minutes later, I was back down in the church basement, keeping busy and *not* coming up with anything good to ask Shuly. But then Father Daniel showed up and did me a major solid.

"Shuly!" he called out across the book sale floor. "You play chess?"

"Yes, sir," she said. "You challenging?"

"Nope," Father Daniel said, and pointed to the chessboard he'd set up on one of the tables in the back. "But Kenny is."

"I am?" I asked.

I looked up from the copy of *Ghost Boys* I was reading, even though I was supposed to be alphabetizing books.

"I mean…sure," I said. Then I went and sat

across the board from Shuly, trying to look like I wasn't shaking in my J's.

Shuly had taken the white pieces and that meant she went first. She started by moving her king's pawn out two spaces.

I moved my queen's bishop pawn two spaces.

"Sicilian Defense, huh?" she asked, and I just looked up at her.

"You know about that?" I asked.

"I might," she said.

In other words, not only was Shuly Williams all that, she also knew a lot about chess. Like she wasn't already perfect enough.

Then she moved a knight.

I moved a bishop.

And it went on from there for a while. We dodged around that board, taking down each other's pieces one by one, until all of a sudden, I saw an opening. And I don't mean for asking Shuly a question. I mean for winning the game.

Shuly's king was in the corner, since she'd castled, and I had one bishop and my own queen blocking her in. All it was going to take was one more move and I'd be right there, at checkmate.

The question was, *Should I do it?*
Would Shuly hate me if I took the win?
Or would she respect me more?
Should I let her have this one?
Or not?

I could feel the doubts creeping into my mind all over again. It was like the Gripper had me in his clutches, freezing my brain and stopping me in my tracks. And of course, all I could think now was—

What would Stainlezz Steel do?

CHAPTER 56

STEEL VS. THE GRIPPER

 **A**s the Gripper moves off into the night, Steel continues to wrestle against the brain worm that sends wave after wave of crippling thoughts through his own mind.

I just lost.

I can't do this.

No use even trying.

Rage and frustration surge through him. He knows that voice in his head isn't real. It's an illusion. Just a digital thought, put there by the Gripper.

But try telling that to his arms and legs.

He wants to stand, but the voice won't let him.

He wants to fly, but his mind says no.

It's a battle of Steel against Steel now. Mind against muscle.

But then, somewhere deep down in the back of his psyche, Steel starts to understand what he has to do.

Don't listen to that voice, he tells himself. *Listen to what you know. Listen to your gut. Your heart. They know what to do.*

It's starting to work, too. Slowly, slowly, Steel

leans forward, onto his knees, and begins to stand up.

Immediately, the brain worm blares even louder in his head, like the Gripper just cranked the volume on him.

WHAT ARE YOU DOING?

YOU CAN'T BEAT THIS, AND YOU KNOW IT!

But Steel isn't listening. Not like before. Now, he's clawing at that titanium nightmare attached to his head and using every bit of strength he can find to pull it away.

GET YOUR HANDS OFF!

LEAVE IT WHERE IT IS!

"You…aren't…real," Steel says out loud.

And saying it makes it a little more true.

A new rush of strength surges through him.

"Steel…" he says. "Steel…is what's…*real.*"

Finally, the head clamp gives way. Steel drags it from his ears and then off his own skull.

Immediately, the thing fights back. It jumps to life like some kind of wild beast in his hands. Steel wrestles it in the air as it tries to fly at his head again. It's freaky strong, too.

But so is Steel.

With every ounce of power he can muster, he twists the demon headgear into a titanium pretzel. Then he crushes the whole thing between his two steel fists and stomps it all to dust on the ground.

So much for the Gripper's brain worm. Now for the Gripper himself.

A tenth of a second later, Steel is flying at maximum speed down the National Mall. His night-vision imaging system has already pinpointed the Gripper's new location.

The Gripper never even sees it coming. Steel scoops him up in one clean pass and flies straight back to the foot of the Washington Monument.

He doesn't stop there, either. Moving at hyperspeed, he flies back and forth, back and forth, using the Gripper himself like a scrubbie, until that paint job starts to disappear.

"Ow, ow, OW, OW!" the Gripper yells the whole time. "Take it easy! I'm just a little guy! Gimme a break!"

"Don't worry," Steel says. "Soon as we're done here, I'll drop you off at the nearest jail cell and you can have all the break you want."

In the meantime, though, there's still plenty of cleaning up to do. Good thing for Steel, he doesn't have anywhere else to be.

CHAPTER 57

STEELING THE GAME

 **S**o there I was, sitting across the chessboard from Shuly and wrestling with my own thoughts about the next move. And for the first time ever, I realized that the thing Steel would do and the thing I would do were exactly the same.

We'd both play to win.

In fact, that's kind of what Father Daniel had said, too. He told me I should be myself. Which means keeping it real. No faking.

So I took my bishop and slid it diagonally two spaces. My hand was shaking, and I thought, *It's not too late, Kenny*. As long as I didn't let go of that chess piece, I could change my mind.

But I didn't. Instead, I let go of the bishop and sat back.

"Checkmate," I said.

Shuly just sat there and looked at the board for a long time.

Then she said, "Well, we should probably get back to helping the ladies." Which sounded a whole lot to me like *HAVE A NICE LIFE, LOSER*.

"But..." she went on. "I want a rematch later."

"YOU DO?" I asked, louder than I meant to. "I mean, you do?"

"That was just a warm-up," Shuly said. "I still need to kick your butt."

And believe me, I've never been so happy to hear someone say that in my life.

"Shuly, why don't you and your mother come over for dinner tonight?" G-ma said. "You two can settle it then."

I hadn't even known G-ma was watching, but now I was glad. It was, like, the coolest thing she'd ever done for me.

"Thanks, Ms. Wright," Shuly said. "I'd love to."

"Yeah, thanks, G-ma," I said.

"You children can thank me by getting back to work on this book sale," G-ma said. Which was more like it, for her.

Not that I was complaining. In fact, I didn't have anything to complain about for the rest of the day. I mean, unless you count the giant mountain of books G-ma bought at the book sale and expected me to carry home.

But even then, at least I had some help this time around. And no, I don't mean from Steel.

CHAPTER 58

UNBELIEVABLE...BUT TRUE

 **W**e'd been biking for a while now, but I wasn't seeing anything familiar. And trying to navigate on a bike through traffic with a phone in your hand is like asking for a broken leg. Or a broken phone. Or a broken bike.

"Any ideas?" I asked Rafe.

"Yeah," he said. "I have an idea that we're lost."

"Me too," I said. Our good luck and bad luck were flipping so fast, I was getting dizzy.

So we pulled over to call Storm. Again.

"Jimmy, please tell me you guys are almost here," she said.

"Why? What's wrong now?" I asked.

"Nothing," she said. "It's just that you're missing the whole thing! Ed Sheeran is on stage!

Ten thousand people are dancing on the Mall!"

I could hear the music in the background and the sound of the crowd going crazy.

"I'm going to drop you a pin to give you my location," I told her. "Maybe Kenny can help me get back. He knows DC better than anyone."

I waited for an answer, but Storm didn't say anything.

"Hello?" I asked.

And then, the weirdest thing happened. The music in the background stopped, really suddenly, but the crowd got even louder. They were screaming and cheering like crazy now.

Rafe couldn't hear any of that, but he still looked confused. "What's going on?" he asked me.

"Storm? What's going on?" I asked.

"I can't believe it," Storm said.

"She can't believe it," I told Rafe.

"Can't believe what?" he asked me.

"Can't believe what?" I asked Storm. "Something good, I hope."

"Something unbelievable," Storm said, and then I heard the audience roar even louder. Whatever this was, it was big.

"Jimmy, listen to me," Storm said. "Stay right where you are. We're coming to get you and, well... you'll see. And I think you're going to like it!"

I was about as confused as a compass in a magnet factory by now. "What do you mean?" I asked.

"I've got to go!" Storm said. "Just stay put! And watch the show on your phone."

"Wait!" I yelled, but she'd already hung up.

"What did she say?" Rafe asked.

"She said to keep watching the show," I said.

So I pulled it up on my phone again, and that's when we saw exactly what was going on.

Storm was right. We *couldn't* believe it. Not even with our own eyes.

And *you* might not believe it either, when I tell you. But you're going to have to wait until after the next story. Because Jamie Grimm was getting ready to take his turn next, and nobody wanted to miss out on that.

CHAPTER 59

HOW DID I GET HERE?

 **H**ave you ever come up with something that seems like a really good idea, until it's time to actually do the thing? And then you're more like, WHAT WAS I THINKING?

Believe me, I'm not afraid of trying new things. Even scary things. Like for instance, getting up on stage in front of an audience and trying to make them laugh. That can be super scary, for sure.

But it's nothing compared to the time I went skydiving.

Yeah, me. The kid in the wheelchair. Don't get too caught up on that part.

The point is, once I was two miles above the

earth in that plane, strapped to my instructor, Rachel, and thinking about free-falling two hundred feet per second on our way back to earth, I was getting a little nervous.

And by a little nervous, I mean really scared.

Okay, more like *absolutely terrified*. Times ten thousand—which is exactly how many feet I had to fall before I was going to be back on solid ground.

"You ready for this?" Rachel shouted in my ear.

"NO!" I yelled back. The plane engines were roaring outside almost as loud as my heart was beating in my chest.

"Well, we're coming up on the jump site. When do you think you might be ready?" she asked me.

"I don't know!" I shouted. "Maybe when I'm thirty?"

But the thing was, I *had* to do this. People were counting on me. I couldn't even call this off if I wanted to. And man, did I want to!

In the meantime, all I could do was try not to think about parachutes with big holes in them, or human bodies flattened like pancakes, while I sat there asking myself over and over, *HOW DID I GET HERE?*

It wasn't a trick question. I knew exactly how I had gotten there.

It was more like I wished I never had.

CHAPTER 60

THE START OF SOMETHING BIG

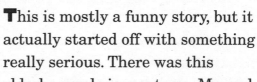**T**his is mostly a funny story, but it actually started off with something really serious. There was this elderly couple in our town, Mr. and Mrs. Campbell, whom everyone liked. Then, on the night of May 9, their house caught fire and they lost almost everything.

It was super sad, except for one thing. And that was the way everyone in town pulled together to help them out. Including me and my friends, Pierce and Gaynor.

The three of us were sitting there at lunch in the cafeteria the next day, talking about what we could do.

"What about a comedy show?" Pierce suggested. "You could do your thing, and people could buy tickets as a fundraiser."

"I don't know," I said, pushing some gray meatloaf around my tray. "I think everyone in town has already seen my act for free. Who's going to pay for it now?"

"Then we have to give them something they've never seen before," Gaynor said.

"I'm not doing it naked!" I said.

That got a laugh, but it also started us thinking.

"Where have you never told jokes before?" Pierce asked.

"Outer space," I said, which was true, even if that wasn't going to happen.

"Where else?" Pierce asked.

"How about the gorilla cage at the zoo?" Gaynor said.

"Aren't gorillas the ones who fling their own poop at people?" I asked.

"I'd pay to see that," Pierce said. But it was a hard *no* for me.

"The top of the Statue of Liberty?" Gaynor suggested.

"Not exactly wheelchair accessible," I said.

"Underwater?" Pierce suggested.

"I don't speak Dolphin," I said. "And I hear sponges have lousy senses of humor."

We were mostly just cracking one another up by now.

"Hey, I know," Gaynor said. "You could jump out of a plane and tell jokes all the way down. Maybe get people to pledge money, like a dollar for every joke you tell while you're in the air."

We laughed at that one, too. "That's hilarious," Pierce said. "I can just see it now."

And then something happened. It was like we all stopped laughing at once and started thinking. *Hmmmmmm.*

I mean, it wasn't like I'd be the first person in a wheelchair to ever go skydiving. I'd seen tons of people doing that online.

But I'd never seen anyone telling jokes on the way down. That was something new. And totally different.

It even seemed like a good idea at the time.

In fact, it seemed like a perfect idea.

Right up until it didn't anymore, but by then, it would be too late to take it back.

CHAPTER 61

SECOND THOUGHTS

 **A**s the day went by, I started thinking about other things. Like what it would be like to actually jump out of an airplane. And what it would be like to crash-land after the parachute didn't work.

You know. Stuff like that.

By the time dinner was over that night, I was starting to realize I'd made a huge mistake. What had I been thinking? I couldn't do this. And I didn't mean because of the wheelchair.

I just meant because...HOW STUPID DO YOU HAVE TO BE TO JUMP OUT OF AN AIRPLANE *ON PURPOSE*?

So I called Gaynor to tell him we needed a new idea.

"Hey," I said when he answered. "I just wanted to tell you—"

But then he cut me off. "Guess what?" he said. "I got Ocean Air Skydiving to donate the jump. And not only that, but I've already put up a KickFunder page, and we have pledges from more than thirty people. We're going to raise at least a thousand bucks, easily!"

"Actually—" I started to say, but Gaynor just kept going.

"I also talked to Mrs. Campbell, and she practically cried when I told her what you were doing for them. She said you're like a hero. A really funny hero."

"Wow," I said. "That's...great."

Because when you're raising money for a family who lost everything, and they already know about it, you can't exactly say, "Ehhh, I don't feel like doing this anymore."

Too late. I was stuck now. The only thing left to do was get myself as ready for this as possible.

I was going to need jokes.

I was going to need courage.

I was going to need me-size diapers.

But you know what they say—one thing at a time.

So I went right into training.

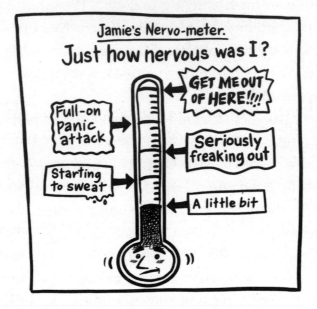

CHAPTER 62

GETTING PUMPED

First, I started lifting. By which I mean the TV remote. I had a whole ton of comedy movies and stand-up specials and old classics I wanted to review.

Then I started doing crunches. And fart sounds. And raspberries. And any other funny noise I could practice ahead of time.

I also hit the treadmill, really hard—right after I went zooming into my uncle's home gym a little too fast with my chair. That's where I keep all my old joke books and journals, and I wanted to see if there was anything I could use in there.

Gaynor and Pierce wanted me to be ready too. Because when I showed up at Pierce's house the next day, they had a whole crazy setup waiting for me in the driveway.

"What is this?" I asked.

"This is your simulator," Pierce said.

There was a lifting bench from Pierce's dad's home gym. They also had a garden hose and a couple of big fans, too.

I was starting to get the idea.

"Come on, let's do this," Pierce said, and handed me a pair of goggles. "Put these on."

After that, I climbed out of my chair and lay on my stomach on the bench. Then Gaynor lay on top of me.

"What are you doing?" I asked.

"I've been watching a bunch of videos," Pierce said. "This is how a tandem jump works. Your instructor will be on your back, wearing the parachute for both of you."

"Yeah, but I can't breathe with Gaynor on top of me," I gasped out.

"That's what the practice is for," Pierce said. "You think it's going to be easy to breathe and tell jokes when you're falling through thin air toward the earth?"

"Okay, okay," I said. I didn't need all the gory details. I was already scared enough as it was. "So I get what the fans are for, but what's with the garden hose?"

"That's for the fake rain, to go with the fake wind."

"They won't let me jump if it's raining," I said.

"Yeah, but it's more fun for us this way," Pierce said, and squirted me in the face. "Okay, start being funny!"

CHAPTER 63

UP, UP, AND...
GET ME OUT OF HERE!

 **F**inally, the really big (and really scary) day arrived. Pierce was true to his word, too. He had a whole crowd at the airstrip to cheer me on. Which was awesome, as long as I didn't go splat right in front of them at the end.

I was excited! For real.

But more than that, I was nervous.

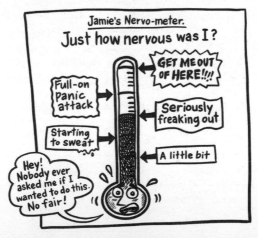

Really, really, really nervous. (But you already knew that, didn't you?)

Now came the *real* training. I met Rachel, my instructor, and she went over everything with me. I'd have her strapped to me like a backpack, so I couldn't lose her if I tried. I'd also have a strap around my legs that she could use to lift my feet up and keep them from dragging as we came in for the landing.

We even practiced getting in and out of the plane that way, while it was still on the ground. Which is kind of like using your stuffed animals as practice for lion taming.

Then before I knew it, Pierce and Gaynor were helping me get into a flight suit, and Rachel was putting more straps around my shoulders, my stomach, my ankles, and I don't even know where else. By the time she was done, I felt like a mummy. The kind of mummy you throw out of airplanes.

I also had a GoPro with a microphone on my helmet, and another camera on a selfie stick with a strap for my wrist so I could record my comedy set on the way down. Which I guess meant I was ready.

Or at least, as ready as I was going to get. Which wasn't much.

"Good luck!" Pierce said, as Rachel helped me get onto the plane.

"Why would you say that?" I asked. "Do you think I'm going to *need* luck?"

"Break a leg!" Gaynor said. That's usually something funny you say to performers before they go on stage instead of wishing them luck, but in this case it was the total *wrong* thing to say.

I started breathing deeply to calm myself. It didn't work. I sounded like a vacuum cleaner.

"He's freaking out," Gaynor noticed.

"He'll be fine," Rachel said.

"Don't worry, Jamie," Pierce said. "The first ten thousand feet are the hardest."

I tried to smile, but mostly I was wondering if that was the last joke I'd ever hear.

Then they slid the airplane door closed, and we took off into the air, to find out one way or another.

CHAPTER 64

FLYING LEAP

**A**s we climbed into the sky, I went over my set list in my head. I had a bunch of new jokes about skydiving and also some of my go-to stuff about school, cafeteria food, and that kind of thing. I wasn't sure how long I'd be up there, so I also had some backup material about pet rabbits ("raisin factories"), another one about brussels sprouts ("little orbs of torture"), and a few about school bullies ("I'm not naming any names, Stevie Kosgrov, but this one's for you").

That helped distract me for a minute, but when I looked up again, we were already getting close to the moment of truth, and I freaked out all over again.

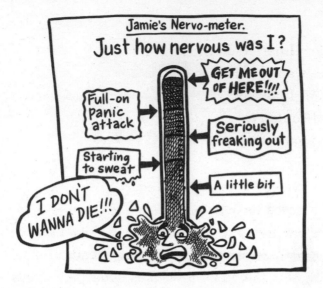

Before I could even say, "I THINK I NEED TO CHANGE MY UNDERWEAR," Rachel was sliding open the side door of the plane.

The wind whipped inside and the noise of the engines got twice as loud. Almost as loud as my heart, which was crowd-surfing through my rib cage by now.

"You've got this!" Rachel yelled in my ear.

I couldn't see her behind me, but I flashed a thumbs-up, only long enough to see my thumb shaking like a palm tree in a hurricane. So I put it away.

I knew I had to do this.

I just wasn't sure I could.

Except I had to.

But I couldn't.

But I had to.

But—

"Here we go!" Rachel shouted.

She scooted us over to the edge of the plane door and swung our legs out. When I looked down, here's what I saw, in this order:

My own two feet.

Another ten thousand feet of air.

Planet Earth.

"Ready?" Rachel shouted.

"NO!" I said, but I don't think she heard me.

"One…" she said, and we rocked a little bit forward. I might have peed a little bit in my flight suit, too.

"Two…" she said, and we rocked back.

"Three!" she said, and this time, we rocked ALL the way forward, just before—

AUUUUUUUGHHHHHHHH
GHHHHHHHHHHHHHHH
GHHHHHHHHHHHHHH
HHHHHHHHHHHHH
HHHHHHHHHHH
HHHHHHHHHHH!!!!

We fell out into the sky.

CHAPTER 65

GOING DOWN

For the first three hours (well, okay, maybe it was about ten seconds), everything was just a blur. I tried to breathe. I tried to think of a joke. I tried to remember my name.

"Hey, everyone," I said into the camera. "It's... it's...it's..."

"Jamie Grimm!" Rachel shouted.

"Right!" I said. "Jamie Grimm!"

I couldn't get my brain to match up with my mouth, which was flapping like a plastic bag in all that wind anyway.

"Just hang on a second!" Rachel shouted.

"For what?" I shouted back.

"For this!"

Then she pulled the rip cord, and everything changed all over again.

I felt a huge tug, and we went flying straight back up. That didn't seem like a good idea, since it just took us farther away from the earth.

"Look up!" Rachel said.

When I did, I saw our bright green parachute over my head, just before we changed directions one more time...

And started to fall again...

But not falling exactly...

More like floating...

Back down toward the ground...

And all of a sudden, it was quieter.

It was floaty.

And it was...

A-MA-ZING.

The whole world was spread out around us, as far as I could see in any direction. It was all weirdly exciting and peaceful at the same time.

I felt tiny.

I felt incredible.

"I feel like I'm flying!" I said.

"That's because you are!" Rachel called back.

"Hey, look, everyone, my *fly* is open!" I said into the camera. "Get it?"

Then I heard Rachel laugh. And just like that, the jokes started to come.

"So like I said, this is Jamie Grimm," I went on. "I'm coming at you from somewhere above LeBron James's head and beneath the sun.

"It looks like we're still about five thousand feet off the ground," I said. "And speaking of five thousand feet, man, does this flight suit stink! It smells like, well…five thousand smelly feet! Who wore this thing before me, the whole Air National Guard?"

Rachel laughed again, and it was like the sound of money. Literally. Every joke I told meant more cash for Mr. and Mrs. Campbell.

So I kept going, as much as I could.

"The good news is, I'm still alive. The bad news is, there's still time for that to change. I mean, it's not as if I've spent the past week thinking about landing like a pancake down there, but…oh, wait. That's exactly what I've been thinking about.

"And speaking of pancakes, how about that cafeteria food at our school, huh?" I asked into the camera. "I mean, seriously. I know those lunches aren't exactly expensive, but isn't it a little like paying for food poisoning?

"I'm not saying there are cockroaches in the cafeteria at my school, but I will say that I've never seen meatballs with tiny little legs before. Mine were so disgusted with the creamed corn at lunch the other day that they got up and walked away."

Rachel liked that one. I heard her cracking up, and I could even feel a smile on my own face.

"Hey, my jump instructor is laughing!" I said. "That seems like a good sign. Studies show that most people don't laugh if they think they're about to become a human crash-test dummy."

As we kept floating down, I kept on joking. My mind was flying too much to keep count, but every joke felt like another dollar sign.

And then before I knew it, the ground was coming up fast. I could see a crowd of people waiting for us, and pretty soon, I could hear them chanting my name, too.

"Ja-mie! Ja-mie! Ja-mie!"

They'd even set up a big target for when we got to the ground, and I pointed my helmet cam at it, which counted as another joke. *Cha-ching!*

"Here we go!" Rachel said. "Coming in for a landing."

She pulled the lines on the chute to slow

us down. That's called a flare. Then she pulled the strap around my legs to keep my feet up as we executed a perfect landing, right on target.

Call me crazy, but I already wanted to go again.

Gaynor and Pierce were right there with my chair. Rachel helped get me un-mummified, and they sat me down while everyone cheered and asked questions.

"How was it?" Gaynor asked.

"Unbelievable!" I said. As in, I literally couldn't believe I'd just done that.

"How many jokes did you tell?" Pierce asked.

"We'll have to go to the instant replay for that," I said.

"Were you scared?" someone else asked.

"Scared?" I said. "Ha! Don't make me laugh!"

Because you know what? Making people laugh is *my* job. Now, more than ever.

And seriously, if you're ever afraid of doing something, and it's not illegal, like robbing a bank, then I say go for it. You might just surprise yourself.

I know I sure did.

CHAPTER 66

NEXT FLIGHT TO WASHINGTON

 **Y**ou might not even believe me when I tell you this next part. I guess I'll leave that up to you. It's a good story, anyway.

So there Rafe and I were, waiting for whoever was going to pick us up in the middle of Washington, DC.

The first thing I noticed was a shadow over my face. Then I looked up and saw two people with giant wings on their backs, headed our way.

Yeah, you heard me.

Giant wings.

Headed our way.

Crazy, right?

"Is that who I think—?" Rafe asked.

"Yep," I said.

"But I thought they—"

"I thought so too," I said.

"So then—"

"I don't know."

My eyes felt like they'd just gotten three times bigger as I watched Maximum Ride and her second in command, Fang, come in for a landing right there on Connecticut Avenue.

People honked, and even more people stared, but these guys knew what they were doing. Max timed her landing perfectly, tucking her wings back as she came to a stop right next to me. Fang did one more loop around and came in for his own landing right behind her.

If you don't know about Maximum Ride, she's got a book named after her, like everyone else on our team. (Just don't get her confused with Max Einstein—the other Max. She's cool too, but only *this* Max can *fly*!)

She's older than me, maybe sixteen, but I'm not sure. Definitely a teenager, anyway, which makes her different from the gang I usually hang out with.

Well, that and the wings, of course.

Max's story is different too. She lives with a whole family of kids with wings like hers. She's the oldest there, which makes her like the cool mom in that group. When I sent her an invitation to our big event on the National Mall, I never really expected her to make it, much less with Fang along for the ride.

"Sorry we're late," she said.

"You're right on time," I said. "I've been missing the whole show. Plus, I have to get a special delivery back to Mrs. Bash."

"Who?" Fang asked.

"Don't worry about it," I said.

"Okay, I won't," Max said. "Besides, we've got to keep moving. You guys ready?"

Rafe's mouth was opening and closing, but nothing was coming out. I think he was more surprised than anyone by this whole thing.

"We're ready," I said. "Right, Rafe?"

He managed to nod, and his eyes got even bigger.

"I'll take that as a yes," Fang said. "Come on, Rafe. Hop on."

"That means you're with me," Max told me.

Besides having awesome wings, Max and her flying friends are way stronger than regular people like me and Rafe. So she didn't mind a bit when I climbed on her back. And Fang basically looked like he was made of muscle and feathers.

"Hang on tight!" Max said. Then she got a running start, unfurled those huge wings of hers, flapped twice, and we had liftoff.

When I looked back, Fang and Rafe were right behind.

"How you doing?" I yelled to Rafe.

"One word!" he yelled back. "WOOOO-HOOOOO!"

So far that day, we'd gone from riding in an Uber, to running on foot, to taking the subway, to traveling by rent-a-bike. Now we were finally going to make it back to the National Mall in style. And I mean crazy, crazy, crazy style.

Believe it or not.

CHAPTER 67

SEEMS LIKE YESTERDAY

 Hi, everyone! I'm so glad to be here, and I want to thank Jimmy for making me an honorary kid for the day. I'm on a break from my latest movie project, and it's my directorial debut. That's right, I'm directing my first movie ever, and I'll tell you about that in a few minutes.

But first, I'm going to share a story with you, all about how I got started in show business. It happened in the town of Seaside Heights, on the boardwalk just a few blocks from the house where I grew up.

In fact, I can remember it like it was yesterday....

"Yesterday, all my troubles seemed so far away...."

That was me, belting out a favorite Beatles tune for the tourists, making a little summer cashola with my guitar.

Hey, it was better than working the cotton candy booth like my sister Victoria, or mowing lawns like my sister Hannah, or babysitting like my sister Riley. (I have a lot of sisters. Six, to be exact.)

It was nice to work outside, get some fresh air

and sunshine, and listen to the sweet *clink-clink-clink* of loose change dropping into my open guitar case as the people walked by. Even better was the soft *swiff* of a dollar bill.

"Yesterday, all my troubles seemed so far away...."

Clink!

"Now it looks as though they're here to stay...."

Clink!

"Oh, I believe in yesterday."

Swiff!

Yes! I liked that nice paper-money sound at the end of a song. But when I looked down, there wasn't a picture of George Washington in sight. Someone had dropped a yellow flyer in my case, and now she was walking away.

"Hey! This isn't your garbage can!" I called after her.

"I didn't think it was," she said. "You're a performer, right?"

"Yeah, what about it?" I asked.

"Look at the flyer," she said, and moved on.

So I picked it up, and boy-oh-boy, am I glad I didn't toss that thing in the trash. Because right there on that flyer, I saw my *whole future* just waiting for me.

It was the moment I'd been working for all my life. This was a chance to be in a real movie, which was my number one dream.

Two seconds later, I'd closed up shop (by which I mean my guitar case) and I was hurrying over to the tent they had set up at the far end of the boardwalk.

Now I just had to nail this audition.

CHAPTER 68

THE AUDITION

 **W**hen I got to the tryouts, there was a long line of people waiting to get in. But I didn't mind. This was all part of it. Making movies! Show business! It was in the air now, like the smell of cotton candy and seawater.

When I finally got to the front of the line, a PA (that means "production assistant") directed me inside the tent, where I found three bored-looking people sitting at a long table.

Which meant it was my job to make sure they didn't look bored by the time I was done.

"Hi! I'm Jacqueline Hart, and I want to be in your movie!" I said. "For my monologue, I will be performing a speech from—"

The guy in the middle held up a hand to stop

me. Even his fingers looked bored.

"We don't need a monologue, kid," he said.

"Oh!" I answered, as cheerful as a daisy. "How about a song, then? 'Yesterday, all my troubles seemed so far away—'"

"Stop!" he said. "Can you walk like a zombie? Because that's what we need for the scene we're shooting tomorrow. Lots and lots of zombies."

"Absolutely!" I said. "Zombies are my specialty!"

Here's something you should know. When someone asks you at an audition if you can do something, the answer is always *YES*.

The truth is, I'd never really thought much about it before. But I *had* dragged myself out of bed on school mornings plenty of times. And that always felt a whole lot like being a zombie.

So I lay down on the ground, closed my eyes, and imagined my alarm clock going off at six in the morning.

"Urghhh…" I said.

I put one arm out from under my imaginary blankets.

"Glarrrhhh…"

Then I stuck out the other arm.

"Errrrrghhhh…"

I dragged myself into a sitting position and stood up, almost like I was sleepwalking. But also— hopefully—like I was zombie-walking.

I imagined myself heading to the bathroom next and shuffled right toward the casting people. I thought about eating one of their faces, which is maybe what a zombie might eat for breakfast.

"Glerrrghhhh…" I said.

"Okay, that'll do," the casting guy told me. "Nice work."

"Nice work"?

"NICE WORK"?

It was like fireworks going off in my head. Because guess what? A HOLLYWOOD CASTING GUY HAD JUST SAID THAT I'D DONE *NICE WORK*! He didn't even look bored anymore.

"Here," one of the two ladies said, and held out a pink sheet of paper. "Take this and bring it back tomorrow at four thirty for makeup and wardrobe."

I couldn't even believe it. Makeup? Wardrobe? Those were such MOVIE-ish words!

"You won't regret this!" I told them. "I'll see you tomorrow afternoon!"

"Guess again," one of the ladies told me. "We need you here at four thirty in the *morning*."

"Oh," I said. "Of course. I knew that."

I wanted to hug them all, but that probably wasn't very professional. So I bowed instead. Then I shook their hands and ran all the way home like my sneakers were made out of hovercrafts on little pink clouds.

Movie life, here I come!

CHAPTER 69

METHOD TO MY MADNESS

 **H**ave you ever heard of method acting? That's when you get so into a part, it's like you're *living* it, not just acting it. And since I couldn't exactly bring myself back from the dead like a real zombie, I did the next best thing.

"Zombie movie party!" I shouted as I came into the house. I'd made a quick stop at the video store (this was back when there was such a thing as video stores) and I'd rented a whole pile of videotapes. "Who's in?"

Once I told my father and my sisters what this was all about, they got as excited as I was. Dad popped a gigantic bowl of popcorn. Sophia went out and bought a huge bag of M&M's to mix in with the popcorn (because there's nothing better than that with a movie), and we all settled in for a zombie marathon.

Well, everyone except for my sister Emma. She was too young for this stuff and was away visiting friends with my mom, anyway.

We started with the all-time great, *Night of the Living Dead*. That movie may be old, but it's *scary*. And there's a reason they call these things classics. If I was going to play a zombie in a movie, I wanted to know how it all started.

After that, Dad, Victoria, and Hannah went off to bed.

"No problem," I said. "More snacks for the rest of us."

I probably should have left the popcorn and M&M's alone, because zombies don't eat anything but human flesh. But I couldn't resist.

Next up, Sophia, Riley, and I watched *Fresh from the Grave*. It was even scarier, and we held on to one another until it was over.

After that, Sophia and Riley were zombie'd out, and they went to bed too. I chugged some Diet Coke to stay awake and popped in a comedy, *Zombie Family Reunion,* just for variety.

While I watched, I stood in front of the TV and imitated all the undead people, slogging back and forth across my living room. I also bit into the couch cushions like they were human victims, just to get a feel for it.

Around 2:00 a.m., I downed some more sugary soda and watched *Tastes Like Chicken.* I couldn't tell if the movies were getting worse or if I was just exhausted. But I pushed through.

By then, it was almost four in the morning. Time to get ready for work!

When I looked in the bathroom mirror, I had dark bags under my eyes. My hair was a mess, and I was practically twitching from all the Diet Coke. Perfect! Now I just had one more little thing to do.

I snuck up to Sophia's room and silently opened the door. Then I zombie-walked across the floor with my arms out in front of me.

"Glarrrrrr…" I said quietly. I could tell the light from the hall was making a silhouette of my body, which was just what I wanted. "GLARRRRR!"

Sophia's eyes popped open, and she screamed bloody murder.

"Did I scare you?" I asked.

"YES, YOU SCARED ME!" she said.

"Oh, good! That's a relief," I said. "Now, wish me luck and go back to sleep."

She only harrumphed and turned over without a word. I guess some people just don't understand show business.

As for me, this was the best day of my life and it wasn't even five in the morning yet. A few seconds later, I was out the door and practicing my zombie shuffle all the way over to the boardwalk for my first day on my first movie, ever!

CHAPTER 70

LiGHTS, CAMERA, ZOMBiES!

**H**ere's something else I haven't told you. In fact, it was the best part of the whole thing.

When I got to the makeup and wardrobe tent with all the other extras, I finally heard about who was playing the lead in this movie.

Duncan Masterson.

The Duncan Masterson.

No big deal. Just my favorite actor, *ever*! If the makeup lady hadn't told me to sit still a thousand times, I would have been jumping out of my chair all morning.

So I tried to keep calm and thought about getting into character. *If I luck out and play my cards right,* I thought, *I might even get to take a fake bite out of Duncan Masterson's arm. Or maybe even pretend-eat a little of his face off.*

* I love you, too, Duncan.

And I had plenty of time to think, too.

Here's another little secret about making movies. It's a *lot* of fun, except when it's slow and boring, which is most of the time. It takes forever to do pretty much anything on a movie set. Including makeup and wardrobe.

They put prosthetic shredded skin on my

forehead and arms. They blackened all around my eyes. They made my lips look like they were mega-chapped. They even put me in a wig that looked like old hay that had been electrocuted. By the time I got out of that makeup chair, I was incredibly ugly—in a totally awesome way.

It was also five hours after I'd gotten to the set.

Then they put us all in a "holding pen," which was just another tent, where we got free doughnuts and waited for another three long hours to shoot the scene.

Finally, we got the call from the second AD (that's "assistant director"), and we filed outside to get started.

"Okay, everyone!" the director told us. "You're hungry zombies. All you care about is getting something to eat. And right now, the only victim in sight is this guy, right here—Blake Zipmore, who of course will be played by the one and only Duncan Masterson!"

That's when Duncan came out of his trailer and everyone cheered. A few people might have even screamed. And yeah, I might have been one of those screamers.

But I also had to pay attention. I wanted to know as much as I could about everything, so I could be at the head of the pack when the scene started. That's how I was going to get noticed.

That's also how I was going to make sure I was on screen in the finished movie.

And most of all, that's how I was going to get close to Duncan Masterson.

CHAPTER 71

AND WE'RE ROLLING!

**O**nce the cameras were rolling, it was even more exciting.

We zombies were all supposed to slowly corner Duncan's character, Blake Zipmore, until he was completely mobbed. Later, they'd shoot the part where he breaks through the boardwalk and escapes into the ocean. But for now, it was just going to be one big zombie pile-on.

I knew I had to stay in character, which meant that I had to move as slowly as a zombie would. But I also had to make sure I was a little faster than the others, so I could be the first to get to Duncan.

It was like an acting challenge. I decided that my zombie hadn't eaten anyone in months, and she was going to be starving. That was her motivation for getting ahead.

"And...ACTION!" the director called out.

We all started shuffling and grunting our way across the boardwalk in a swarm. I kept thinking, *Zombie, zombie, zombie,* to keep myself focused. But I also kept thinking, *Duncan, Duncan, Duncan.* I couldn't help it. He was right there in front of us.

And in fact, it was working. Because as I came close, I couldn't see any other zombies to my left or right. All I could really see was Duncan, and those pretty brown eyes of his—

"CUT!" The director's voice came over a bullhorn. "Let's lose the speed demon, please!"

When I stopped and looked around, I realized I'd left the zombie pack in the dust, and they were all looking my way. In other words, the speed demon was *me.*

"I'm sorry!" I said. "I guess I got a little excited."

"Let's go again!" the AD shouted. "Everyone back to one, please." That meant we were supposed to go back to our starting positions.

I promised myself not to move too fast this time. But I didn't want to go too slowly, either. I couldn't afford to get lost in the crowd.

"Everyone settle, please!" the director yelled. "And...ACTION!"

We started again, and this time, I made sure

to stay with the group. I was near the front but not way out ahead. Which was perfect. Duncan was doing his part too, as he backed up against the fence around the merry-go-round. He looked terrified, in a handsome and rugged kind of way. I don't think anyone has ever looked that good being hunted by the undead before. It was actually kind of adorable—

"CUT! CUT! CUT!" someone yelled.

We all looked over at the director. And once again, he was looking right back at me.

"Zombies don't grin!" he said, to me. "What in the world are you smiling about?"

I could feel myself blushing under all that makeup. Even Duncan Masterson was staring, and not in a good way.

"I'm so sorry!" I said. "I promise I'll get it right—"

"Yeah, thank you very much. That'll be all," the director snapped. "Bucky, can you show our little smiling speed demon the way out, please?"

"What?" I said. "Wait...what?"

Was I being fired?

I mean, I knew I was being fired. But I couldn't believe it. As fast as this opportunity had fallen in my lap, now it was being taken away. And the best day of my life had just turned into the worst one ever.

Just like a big Hollywood flop.

Without the Hollywood part.

CHAPTER 72

BACK TO ONE

"Yesterday, all my troubles seemed so far away. Now it looks as though they're here to stay. Oh, I believe in yesterday...."

That was me, back out on the boardwalk trying to make some money again. I had to, now that my movie career had crashed and burned so quickly.

It was the end of the day, and I hadn't been able to get anywhere near that closed movie set. I missed the whole thing.

So I just poured my heart into my music and tried not to think about it. Right up until I heard the familiar *swiff* of a dollar bill falling into my case.

When I looked down, I saw that it wasn't just a one-dollar bill, but a *twenty*. And when I looked up,

I saw that it wasn't just anyone who'd dropped it there, but Duncan Masterson.

DUNCAN.

FREAKING.

MASTERSON!

"Sorry about what happened to you on set today," he said.

After I picked up my chin off the boardwalk, I managed to answer him.

"It's not your fault," I said. "It was mine. But hang on. How did you even know it was me?"

"I wouldn't have recognized you out of your makeup, but I recognized your voice," he said. "And for the record, you were a darn good zombie."

I blushed all the way to the sky on that one. It was like getting an instant sunburn.

"You're just being nice," I said. "The truth is, I was trying way too hard."

"When people try too hard, it usually means they care about what they're doing," he said. "And those are the people who make it in this business."

"Really?" I asked.

"It doesn't mean everything's always going to

work out, but if you don't push it a little, you don't get anywhere," he said.

"Yeah, well, I got somewhere, all right," I said. "All the way to the exit."

"You know what my mom used to say to me?" he asked.

I couldn't believe I was having an actual conversation with Duncan Masterson. It was even better than getting to pretend-eat his face off. He was so nice and had such a warm smile—

"Hello?" Duncan waved a hand in front of my face. "Anyone there?"

"Oh! Sorry!" I said. "What did your mom always say to you?"

"She said, 'Just keep failing until you don't,'" he told me. "In fact, when I was starting, I tried out for about a hundred movies before I even got one tiny part."

"Seriously?" I asked, and he nodded. That was a surprise to hear. I mean, what kind of idiots wouldn't want *the* Duncan Masterson in their movies?

But I guess that was the point. He wasn't always *the* Duncan Masterson. And maybe with a little luck, and a lot of failing along the way, I could someday be *the* Jacky Hart.

I definitely had one gigantic failure under my belt already. So maybe that was a start.

And guess what? Here's the kicker to my story. It all happened about twenty years ago. And do you remember how I told you I was in the middle of directing my first movie right now? Well, just guess who's playing one of the lead roles.

Go on, guess.

But then again, maybe you don't have to.

CHAPTER 74

NEW BOT IN TOWN

I have a surprise for you," Mom said as she set a brand-new bot on the living room floor. He looked like a backpack with legs. But also like a crab. And maybe a little like a vacuum cleaner, too.

"Who's this?" I asked, because in our house, robots aren't *whats*. They're *whos*.

"Sammy, this is Victor Ricardo," Mom said.

"Hello, Sammy," he said, in a very human-sounding voice. "Would you like to begin?"

One of the cool things about having a genius inventor for a mom is that I get to try out all her new stuff. Which I guess makes me the family guinea pig.

"Sure!" I said. "What are we doing?"

"Please hold," he said, and started walking toward me.

"Why did you name him Victor Ricardo?" I asked Mom.

"You'll see," she said.

First, he climbed onto my back and held on with two of his crablike legs. Next, a green glass screen wrapped around my eyes. I could still see the living room, but there was a holographic menu hanging in front of me now too.

"Ohhh, I get it," I said to Mom. "Victor Ricardo. Like VR."

"I am the most advanced virtual reality player ever created," Victor Ricardo said. "I can take you anywhere you want to go without even leaving the house."

"Cool. Let's start at the top," I said. Then I reached out and "touched" the virtual button for Adventure.

"Good choice," he said.

Suddenly, the whole living room around me slid away as a redwood forest slid into view. I looked up and saw the tallest trees I'd ever seen. I could hear a river running nearby. I could even feel a breeze on my face.

It was all so...real. Or at least...virtually real.

"I can offer you hundreds of options," Victor Ricardo said. "For instance..."

Just like that, the forest evaporated and I was standing on the rim of the Grand Canyon. I almost fell in before I remembered I was still in my living room.

"WHOA!" I yelled.

"There's more," Victor Ricardo told me, as the

Grand Canyon morphed into sand dunes like skyscrapers on either side of me.

"The Sahara is quite nice this time of year," he said. "Or maybe you'd prefer something like this."

All that sand turned into blue water, and I found myself at the bottom of the ocean.

"Or this?"

Just like that, I was surrounded by stars, planets, and galaxies in every direction.

That's when I knew it was about to turn into a *very* interesting afternoon.

And it did, for sure. But not in the way I'd thought!

CHAPTER 75

JEALOUS MUCH?

 How do I even decide where to go?" I asked.

"You should go to the moon," Mom told me. "That's one of my favorites."

"I can do that?" I asked.

"Absolutely," Victor Ricardo said.

In another blink, I was sitting inside my new spacecraft. I could see a LAUNCH button on the giant control panel in front of me. I could hear the engines humming.

"Wow!" I said. "This is all totally next-level stuff."

"There's more," Mom said. "Victor Ricardo also has a higher PQ than any bot I've worked on."

"PQ?" I asked.

"Personality quotient," Mom told me. "You've

been saying my bots need more personality. So I bumped it all the way up this time."

"And please, call me Vic," he said. "I am an operating system and a friend, all in one. Once you see what I can do, you will have no need for any other bot."

From the doorway, I heard the sound of grinding gears. That's how my friend E clears his throat to let you know he's there.

E is like my brother, but the robotic kind. He goes to school with me, and rides bikes with me, and does pretty much everything else I do. Mom invented him, too.

"Hey, E!" I said. "You want to go to the moon?"

"I'd be delighted!" E said.

"E is not necessary to this adventure," Vic said.

"I didn't say he was necessary," I told Vic. "I just asked if he wanted to come."

I think I heard Vic grumble. Which was weird. It was like he was jealous or something.

"Very well," Vic said. "E, you can log in through the home Wi-Fi."

"I knew that," E said, a little defensively. "I wasn't fabricated yesterday."

"Come on, you two, play nice," Mom told them.

I heard a whirring sound and E shimmered into view, right next to me. I knew we were both still in the living room at home, but all I could see around me was that space capsule, waiting to take off.

"How strange," E said. "I've never been a virtual version of myself."

"There's probably a lot you haven't seen," Vic said. "My sensors tell me you're an older model."

"Vic, be polite," Mom said. "You two are going to have to get along."

"I'm sorry," Vic said. "By all means, E, come right in. Enjoy yourself."

"Much better," Mom said. "Sammy, I'll be in my lab if you need anything. Have fun!"

"Thanks, Mom!" I said as she went back to work. "E, you ready to launch?"

"I believe so," E said.

"Well, try to keep up," Vic said. "I mean, if you can...old man."

It was like as soon as Mom left the room, Vic went back to his rude self. *Maybe that's part of the high PQ Mom talked about,* I thought. I mean, being a jerk is *kind of* like having a personality, right?

Mostly, though, I couldn't wait to get going. So I reached out and touched that big LAUNCH button.

"Initiating launch sequence," Vic said. "Here we go!"

I felt a rumbling in my chest as the ship's engines fired up. Then I felt the start of something like g-force as we lifted off and picked up speed. Outside the ship's porthole, I could see blue sky, then clouds, then more sky, before we burned through the atmosphere and straight into the blackness of outer space.

It seemed like we were off to a great start. And it's not like any of it was actually *real*. So what could possibly go wrong now?

The precise answer is...A LOT.

CHAPTER 76

GET OUT

 **I** don't suppose we can do zero gravity?" I asked Vic, once we were on our way.

"Perhaps with a future upgrade to my software," Vic said. "After all, I *am* the most advanced VR system in the universe."

"What a show-off," E muttered. "I'll bet he can't even ride a bike."

"And I would wager that you can't even make a shooting star go by," Vic said, just before a bright white comet filled the ship with light as it went by.

I have to admit, it was pretty cool. But still—

"Stop fighting, you guys," I said. "This is supposed to be fun."

Seriously, sometimes robots are more work than real people.

"We will be entering our orbit around the moon in approximately two minutes," Vic said.

"Perfect," I said. "Let's do a lap all the way around and find somewhere cool to land."

"No problem," Vic said. "Might I suggest the Copernicus crater?"

"Might I suggest the Copernicus crater?" E said in a mocking voice I'd never heard before.

"Be quiet!" Vic said. "You are unnecessary to this exchange."

"BOTH of you be quiet!" I said. But nobody was listening to me.

"Listen here, you crab-walking excuse of a video game," E said. "We've all done quite well without you up to now."

"I guess you'd know, with your multiterabyte processor and unlimited access memory," Vic said. "Oh, wait, no. That's me. Not you."

It was getting ridiculous. I was starting to feel like a dad with two fighting kids in the backseat.

"You're just an overrated Xbox," E said. "I'm the one who is indispensable to this family."

"Do you wish to bet on that?" Vic asked.

"I do not make bets," E said.

"Well, let's find out just how indispensable you are," Vic said. "Initiating ejection sequence."

"Hang on," I said. "What does that mean?"

A red light on the console in front of me started flashing.

"Standing by for ejection in ten, nine, eight…"
Vic started counting down.

"Vic, what are you doing?" I yelled.

"I'm merely making a point," he said.

"Well, stop making it!" I said.

"I'm sorry, but I do not recognize that command string," Vic said. "Five, four…"

"E? Can you override this system?"

"I'm trying!" E said. "What's the password for this thing?"

"Mom didn't tell me!"

"Three, two, one," Vic finished counting down.

"Sammy?" E hollered.

"And…eject!" Vic said.

I looked over, and even though I knew the real E was sitting on the couch next to me, what I saw inside that spaceship was the ceiling hatch popping open. Followed immediately by E shooting right out of that ship like a piece of toast from an intergalactic toaster.

"E!" I shouted.

I reached for him, but it was too late. He was already gone, gone, gone.

CHAPTER 77

GONE

VIC!" I yelled. "What did you do that for?"

"I was simply proving my point," Vic answered. "E said he was indispensable. I said he was not. As it turns out, I was correct."

"That's it—I'm out of here," I said. I pulled the screen away from my face and looked around. "Come on, E. Let's go do something else."

E was sitting there on the couch next to me. But now his eyes were dark, like he'd powered down. Or gone into a robot trance.

"E?" I asked. "E!"

"E is still inside the game," Vic said calmly.

"Well, get him back!" I said.

"I'm afraid I can't, Sammy," Vic told me. "E logged himself in. Which means we'll have to retrieve him from inside the game."

"Can't you just reboot, or shut down, or something?" I asked.

"I wouldn't suggest that," Vic said. "In order to experience the enhanced virtual reality, E's operating system and 98 percent of his memory have been uploaded to my servers. You could certainly retrieve the physical being on your couch, but E would be null at that point."

"Null?" I asked.

"I believe the phrase 'robot zombie' might apply here," Vic said.

I couldn't believe this. Then again, weird stuff happens in my house all the time.

"So in other words, if I want to get E out of the game, I have to go back in," I said.

"Precisely."

"Why didn't you tell me that before?" I asked.

"It's never come up before," Vic answered.

"Of course it hasn't!" I shouted. "You're a brand-new bot!"

"Well, yes," Vic said. "Good point. But I'll certainly remember that next time."

"Fine. Whatever!" I said, and pulled the VR mask back over my eyes. "Come on. Let's go find E."

CHAPTER 78

SPACE CATCH

The good news was, my mom was a real scientific genius. That meant that even inside this game, virtual outer space would behave like the real thing. Once E left the ship, he'd keep traveling in the same direction until something—or someone— stopped him.

The bad news was, we still had to catch up with him. It wasn't just like a grab-and-go. More like looking for a needle in a million haystacks.

But the other good news was, that's not nearly as hard as it sounds when you have a bot doing the calculations.

"I anticipate we'll overtake E in three minutes," Vic told me. We were really flying now. It was like stuff-streaking-past-the-portholes fast, which would have been a whole lot cooler if I wasn't riding shotgun with the world's most annoying artificial intelligence.

"I think you'll be pleased with the rescue apparatus I've loaded into the ship's design. It's quite something, if I do say so myself—"

"I'm not talking to you," I said.

It seemed like we had been going forever before I finally got a trace on E. He showed up as a green blip on a radar screen in front of me.

"E? Can you hear me?" I asked.

"Aug-eegh-joink—I…hear…you," his voice came back.

"Lock in on that signal," I told Vic. "And no funny business."

"Locking in," Vic said, even though he sounded a little disappointed.

And then I could see E, straight ahead. He was spinning and spinning through space like an interplanetary windmill. Made out of a robot.

"We've got you, E!" I shouted. "Vic, slow us down! Reverse thrusters, or…whatever you're supposed to do."

We were coming in too hot, and a second later,

we went shooting right by E.

"Waaaaaaaaiiiiiiit fooooooooooooooor meeeeeeeeeee!" E yelled as we passed him by.

"Just kidding," Vic said.

"Not funny!" E shouted as I felt the whole ship turn a quick one-eighty. A second later, we were headed back the way we'd just come.

"Slower this time!" I said.

Still, I could tell we were going to go right past him again. But I knew what to do.

"Open the hatch," I said. "I'm going out."

I can't take credit for that idea. I stole it from a movie, but at least I knew what to do. I had Vic hook my virtual space suit to a virtual line on a long spool—hopefully long enough to catch E as we went by.

"Here I come, E!" I said.

Then I swan dove straight out of the ship until there was nothing above me, below me, or on either side but endless black space and stars and more stars. If I hadn't been so mad at Vic, I would have told him how INCREDIBLY AWESOME the game part of all this was. But meanwhile—

"YOU'RE GOING TO MISS!" E yelled.

"I'M NOT GOING TO MISS!" I told him.

And then—*OOF!*—we collided in midair. Or is it midspace? Either way, I grabbed on and held him tight. It all felt super real, but I can only imagine how weird it must have looked from the outside.

Just an average day in the Hayes-Rodriguez house.

"Vic, pull us back in!" I yelled.

"Promise you won't shut me down when this is all over," Vic said.

"I promise!" I said.

Well, okay, I lied. But what choice did I have?

Then I felt a tug, and suddenly we were being towed back to the ship.

"How are you holding up, E?" I asked.

"I...don't...like...this...game!" he said, just before we passed through the hatch and were inside again. *Phew!*

"Go ahead and off-load yourself," I told E. "I'll see you back on the couch. And Vic? You can close out this game for good."

"What?" Vic asked. "But we haven't even been to the moon yet—"

"Close enough," I said.

As soon as we'd powered down, I ripped my headgear off and found E wide-awake on the couch next to me. I might have even hugged him.

"What happened?" E asked. "My memory log seems to be wiped for the past thirty-two minutes. How odd."

"You can blame this guy," I said, taking Vic off my back and setting him on the floor.

"Hello, I'm E," he said to Vic.

"Nice to meet you," Vic said.

"Don't even try," I told him.

"Wait, I can explain!" Vic said, as I reached for his main power switch.

"Sweet dreams," I said.

"No...don't...wait—"

CLICK.

And just like that, it was game over.

CHAPTER 79

BACK TO THE DRAWING BOARD

CLUNK!

That was the sound of me dropping Vic onto the workbench in Mom's lab a minute later.

"How'd it go?" Mom asked.

"I'd give the VR a ten out of ten," I said. "But this guy needs a little less PQ, if you ask me. It turns out, Vic is the jealous type."

"Fascinating," Mom said.

"Not really," I said.

"Well, let's see what we can do."

So E and I went out for a bike ride. When we got home again, Mom was already waiting for us—with Vic.

"It didn't take long to make the adjustments,"

she said. "See for yourself." Then she pressed a button on Vic's back.

"Good afternoon, everyone," he said. He sounded different this time. Maybe a little nicer. "Shall we begin?"

"What do you think, honey?" Mom asked. "Want to give it another shot?"

I looked over at E, and he looked back at me.

"If at first you don't succeed," E said, "moon, moon again."

That's his version of a little joke. (Very little.)

"Sounds good to me," I said, so we went off to the living room to get another shot at our moon shot. I may not have trusted Vic just yet, but I trusted Mom to have made him better.

Mom always says that genius isn't about knowing all the answers. It's about knowing how to figure them out. That's how this stuff works—one step at a time.

And by the way, if you're ever lucky enough to meet Victor Ricardo (2.0), you should totally ask him to take you to the Copernicus crater on the moon. It's really worth the trip, and trust me, you won't be sorry.

I know I wasn't.

The flag in the image reads: "Sammy and E were (virtually) here"

CHAPTER 80

MAXIMUM IMPACT

 **L**et me tell you something. If you've never flown over Washington, DC, on the back of a friend with giant wings and then come in for a landing on the National Mall while ten thousand people cheer, you are missing OUT!

Yeah, I know how lucky I am. I have the coolest friends in the world.

"We're baaaaaack!" I said, as soon as Max, Fang, Rafe, and I had run over to center stage. "Ladies and gentlemen, give it up for Maximum Ride and Fang!"

All those ten thousand people cheered even louder, if that was possible.

"And how about another round of applause for my buddy Rafe?" I said, holding his hand up with mine, like we were a couple of heavyweight champions. "I never would have made it back here without his help, that's for sure. Rafe, you want to say anything?"

Rafe leaned into the microphone. "Whatever my sister told you about me while I was gone, don't believe a word of it," he said. "Because here's what really happened—"

But then we got swallowed up by Storm, and David, and Jacky, and Kenny, and pretty much everyone from the show. They were pouring onto the stage now, slapping me on the back, shaking Rafe's hand, and congratulating Max and Fang on the excellent entrance they'd just made.

"That was amazing!" Kenny said.

"No," Jamie said. "That was *fly*! Get it?"

"You guys really saved the day, Max," I told her. "Nobody's going to forget what you did for us. I know I won't."

"No sweat," Max said.

"Well, maybe a little sweat," I said. "And I appreciate it." I don't think she'd ever been a human shuttle before.

"Can you guys stick around to tell a story?" Storm asked.

Fang kind of grunted at that. He's not a big talker, but I think that meant no. And I knew what Max would say anyway. If you've read any of her stuff, you know it's not easy being the world's only flying kids. There's always *someone* out to get them. Which is why they never stay in one place for long.

"Wish we could hang, but we've got to go," she said. "Jimmy, you know where to find me if you need me."

And I did. But I'm not telling where. That part's a secret.

So we all stepped back to make some room while she and Fang took off running. When they hit the edge of the stage, they jumped straight out and opened their wings at the same time. They flapped once and whooshed over the audience's heads. They flapped again and this time banked straight up. With one more fast loop around, they pointed themselves west and headed out over the roofs of Washington, DC. A few seconds after that, they disappeared without a trace. Almost like they'd never been there at all.

Thanks again, Max and Fang.

Catch you on the upside.

CHAPTER 81

CHAIN OF COMMAND

Jimmy, look at this!" Storm said. She pointed at her laptop and started flipping from window to window.

"That little flyover from Max and Fang is *exploding* on the internet already."

It was amazing how fast word had gotten out. Tweets, pictures, and videos were pouring into our Twitter and Instagram feeds. Networks and news channels that hadn't even been covering the show were all live-streaming us now. And messages were coming in from everywhere.

"We've already heard from the prime minister of Canada, the first lady of Kenya, and the UN ambassador to Argentina," Storm said. "Everyone wants to know how they can put on a show like this one."

"Awesome!" Beck said.

"We're megafamous!" Georgia said.

"Where's Argentina?" David asked.

My head was spinning. This whole thing had just gone from big...to bigger...to GLOBAL, just like that.

Which meant more people than ever hearing our stories.

Which meant more kids *reading* stories.

Which was the whole idea to begin with.

And weirdly enough, I had Mrs. Bash to thank for that. If she hadn't made me go get that new permit, I never would have gotten lost. And if I hadn't gotten lost, Maximum Ride wouldn't have had to come get me. And if Max hadn't done that, we wouldn't be going worldwide right now.

"I have the London *Times* on the phone," Storm told me. "Can you give them a comment?"

"Ask them to hold for a second," I said. "I still have to get this paperwork to Mrs. Bash."

"We also have a news crew here from CNN," Storm said.

"Jacky and Jamie can handle that one," I said.

"And there's a vlogger from YouTube who wants an interview."

"Ask Georgia to take care of it," I said, just before I finally reached Mrs. Bash in the wings.

"Here you go!" I said, and put that new permit right in her hand. "So I guess we're good to go now, right?"

"Not so fast," Mrs. Bash said.

I didn't like the sound of that. "Is there a problem?" I asked.

"Your grace period, and the *final* warning I gave you, ran out"—Mrs. Bash looked down at that watch of hers—"six and a half minutes ago."

"But I took an Uber! And a subway! And a bike! And a flying girl, just to get back here. You can't be serious," I said.

Except she was. *Seriously* serious. In fact, she tore that new permit into little pieces, right there in front of me.

"I have been bending the rules for you all day," Mrs. Bash said. "But I will *not* break them. Enough is enough. You need to start sending all these people home."

"Hey, Jimmy?" Storm asked. "You have a FaceTime call coming in."

"Not now," I said. "Mrs. Bash, please! There must be a supervisor or someone I can talk to."

She just shook her head. "I work for the U.S. government," she said. "So technically, my supervisor is—"

"JIMMY!" Storm interrupted again. "Trust me. You *want* to take this call."

"Right now?" I asked.

"Yeah. *Right now,*" Storm said. "In fact, I'm going to put it up on the big screen."

She tapped a bunch of keys on her laptop, and we all looked at the jumbotron. And right there, in front of everyone, was the president of the United States herself.

Yeah, that's right. President Madeline Cooper, leader of the free world, was smiling and waving down at us from that four-story-high screen.

"Hello, my fellow Americans! And hello, all you storytellers out there!" the president said.

"Hello, Madam President!" I said, after my head stopped exploding on the inside. "How can we help you?"

"By continuing to do what you're doing!" she said. "Let's just say I'm a fan."

"Wow, that means a lot," I said. "Thank you!"

"There's more," the president said. "I'm declaring this to be National Storytelling Day, so I hope you're up for doing this again next year. Because I think it should be an annual celebration."

"No way!" said Rafe.

"Way!" said the president.

"We'd be happy to do that, ma'am," I said. "There's just one problem."

That's when I turned Storm's phone to get a shot of Mrs. Bash.

"Madam President, this is Violet Bash from the Washington Association of Special Permits," I said. "She just told me that we're going to have to shut down early because I was six minutes late with our permit."

"Well, I think we can probably do something about that," the president said. "What do *you* say, Mrs. Bash?"

Mrs. Bash's mouth opened and closed about five times before actual words came out.

"I, uh…well…of course, Madam President," she said. "After all, I do work for the U.S. government, which means—"

"It means you work for me," President Cooper said.

"Yes," Mrs. Bash said. "Technically, I believe you are my boss's boss's boss's boss."

"In which case, I'm also closing the W.A.S.P. office for the rest of the day. I hereby order you and your staff to take the afternoon off. Relax a little, Mrs. Bash. Maybe even read a good book," the president told her.

"Well, how can I say no to that?" Mrs. Bash asked.

"You can't," the president said. "And, Jimmy?"

"Yes, ma'am?" I asked.

"You all keep doing what you're doing."

"Yes, ma'am!" I said. "We will! With pleasure."

And I meant that too, of course.

Lots and lots and lots of pleasure.

CHAPTER 82

(NOT) THE END

 **N**ow it was my turn.

Before anything else happened, I stepped back up to the mic in the middle of the stage.

"Have I got a story for you!" I told the crowd.

And I told them all about the day Rafe and I had just had. Because the truth was, I'd never lived through a crazier story in my life.

Not only that, but it wasn't over yet. We had kids lined up all over the National Mall, waiting to tell their own tales at our open-mic stations. We had more musical guests ready to rock the socks off that place. And this time, I wasn't going to miss a second.

So let's not say, *THE END,* here. Let's just say, *What's next?*

Because that's the great thing about stories, and reading, and books. Every time you finish one, there's always another out there just waiting for you to dive right in.

So what are you waiting for? You just finished this one, right?

Go find another!

And another.

And another.

And another.

And another.

GET YOUR PAWS ON THE
HILARIOUS DOG DIARIES SERIES!

Read the Middle School series

Visit the **Middle School world** on the Penguin website
to find out more! **www.penguin.co.uk**

THE

SERIES

THE WORST YEARS OF MY LIFE
(with Chris Tebbetts)
This is the insane story of my first year at middle school,
when I, Rafe Khatchadorian, took on a real-life bear (sort of),
sold my soul to the school bully, and fell for the most popular
girl in school. Come join me, if you dare...

GET ME OUT OF HERE!
(with Chris Tebbetts)
We've moved to the big city, where I'm going to a super-fancy
art school. The first project is to create something based on
our exciting lives. But my life is TOTALLY BORING.
It's time for Operation Get a Life.

MY BROTHER IS A BIG, FAT LIAR
(with Lisa Papademetriou)
So you've heard all about my big brother, Rafe, and now it's
time to set the record straight. (Almost) EVERYTHING he
says is a Big, Fat Lie. I'm Georgia, and it's time for some
payback...Khatchadorian style.

HOW I SURVIVED BULLIES, BROCCOLI, AND SNAKE HILL
(with Chris Tebbetts)

I'm excited for a fun summer at camp—until I find out it's a summer *school* camp. There's no fun and games here, just a whole lotta trouble!

ULTIMATE SHOWDOWN
(with Julia Bergen)

Who would have thought that we—Rafe and Georgia— would ever agree on anything? That's right—we're writing a book together. And the best part? We want you to be part of the fun too!

SAVE RAFE!
(with Chris Tebbetts)

I'm in worse trouble than ever! I need to survive a gut-bustingly impossible outdoor excursion so I can return to school next year. But will I get through in one piece?

JUST MY ROTTEN LUCK
(with Chris Tebbetts)

I'm heading back to Hills Village Middle School, but only if I take "special" classes... If that wasn't bad enough, when I somehow land a place on the school football team, I find myself playing alongside the biggest bully in school, Miller the Killer!

DOG'S BEST FRIEND
(with Chris Tebbetts)
It's a dog-eat-dog world. When I start my own dog-walking empire, I didn't think it could go so horribly wrong! Somehow, I always seem to end up in deep doo-doo...

ESCAPE TO AUSTRALIA
(with Martin Chatterton)
I just won an all-expenses paid trip of a lifetime to Australia. But here's the bad news: I MIGHT NOT MAKE IT OUT ALIVE!

FROM HERO TO ZERO
(with Chris Tebbetts)
I'm going on the class trip of a lifetime! What could possibly go wrong? I've spent all of middle school being chased by Miller the Killer, but on this trip, there's NOWHERE TO RUN!

BORN TO ROCK
(with Chris Tebbetts)
My brother, Rafe Khatchadorian, has been public enemy #1 my whole life. But if I want to win the Battle of the Bands, I'm going to have to recruit the most devious person I know...

ALSO BY JAMES PATTERSON

THE I FUNNY SERIES
I Funny (*with Chris Grabenstein*)
I Even Funnier (*with Chris Grabenstein*)
I Totally Funniest (*with Chris Grabenstein*)
I Funny TV (*with Chris Grabenstein*)
School of Laughs (*with Chris Grabenstein*)
The Nerdiest, Wimpiest, Dorkiest I Funny Ever
(*with Chris Grabenstein*)

MAX EINSTEIN SERIES
The Genius Experiment (*with Chris Grabenstein*)
Rebels with a Cause (*with Chris Grabenstein*)

DOG DIARIES SERIES
Dog Diaries (*with Steven Butler*)
Happy Howlidays! (*with Steven Butler*)
Mission Impawsible (*with Steven Butler*)
Curse of the Mystery Mutt (*with Steven Butler*)

TREASURE HUNTERS SERIES
Treasure Hunters (*with Chris Grabenstein*)
Danger Down the Nile (*with Chris Grabenstein*)
Secret of the Forbidden City (*with Chris Grabenstein*)
Peril at the Top of the World (*with Chris Grabenstein*)
Quest for the City of Gold (*with Chris Grabenstein*)
All-American Adventure (*with Chris Grabenstein*)

HOUSE OF ROBOTS SERIES
House of Robots (*with Chris Grabenstein*)
Robots Go Wild! (*with Chris Grabenstein*)
Robot Revolution (*with Chris Grabenstein*)

JACKY HA-HA SERIES
Jacky Ha-Ha (*with Chris Grabenstein*)
My Life is a Joke (*with Chris Grabenstein*)

OTHER ILLUSTRATED NOVELS
Kenny Wright: Superhero (*with Chris Tebbetts*)
Homeroom Diaries (*with Lisa Papademetriou*)
Word of Mouse (*with Chris Grabenstein*)
Pottymouth and Stoopid (*with Chris Grabenstein*)
Laugh Out Loud (*with Chris Grabenstein*)
Not So Normal Norbert (*with Joey Green*)
Unbelievably Boring Bart (*with Duane Swierczynski*)
Katt vs. Dogg (*with Chris Grabenstein*)

For more information about James Patterson's novels,
visit www.penguin.co.uk